Be sure to look up the reading group
discussion questions at the end of the book!

* * *

"I've wanted to do this since I met you," Brady said.

He stole another kiss from Libby's mouth, and
then another.

"It isn't that long ago," she answered. Couldn't
even think, at the moment. Felt like hours…or like
months. It wasn't *relevant* somehow.

"Seems longer. Seems…intense." He kissed her hair
and her temples, coaxing her to give him her mouth
once more. Libby didn't want to give it yet. She
still needed the sound of his breathing, his heart.

"It has been, Brady. In a lot of ways, we jumped
in at the deep end because of the girls. Are we just
feeling like this because our daughters are twins?"

"That's too complicated, isn't it?" he said slowly,
at last.

It probably was. He was right.

But nothing that was happening tonight felt
complicated. It felt simple. A man and a woman,
and chemistry so strong it was like a sorcerer's
spell.

Dear Reader,

Step into warm and wonderful July with six emotional stories from Silhouette Special Edition. This month is full of heart-thumping drama, healing love and plenty of babies!

I'm thrilled to feature our READERS' RING selection, *Balancing Act* (SE#1552), by veteran Mills & Boon and Silhouette Romance author Lilian Darcy. This talented Australian writer delights us with a complex tale of a couple marrying for the sake of their twin daughters, who were separated at birth. The twins and parents are newly reunited in this tender and thought-provoking read. Don't miss it!

Sherryl Woods hooks readers with this next romance from her miniseries, THE DEVANEYS. In *Patrick's Destiny* (SE#1549), an embittered hero falls in love with a gentle woman who helps him heal a rift with his family. Return to the latest branch of popular miniseries, MONTANA MAVERICKS: THE KINGSLEYS, with *Moon Over Montana* (SE#1550) by Jackie Merritt. Here, an art teacher can't help but *moon over* a rugged carpenter who renovates her apartment—and happens to be good with his hands!

We are happy to introduce a multiple-baby-focused series, MANHATTAN MULTIPLES, launched by Marie Ferrarella with *And Babies Make Four* (SE#1551), which relates how a hardheaded businessman and a sweet-natured assistant, who loved each other in high school, reunite many years later and dive into parenthood. *His Brother's Baby* (SE#1553) by Laurie Campbell is the dramatic tale of a woman determined to take care of herself and her baby girl, but what happens when her baby's handsome uncle falls onto her path? In *She's Expecting* (SE#1554) by Barbara McMahon, an ambitious hero is wildly attracted to his new secretary—his new *pregnant* secretary—but steels himself from mixing business with pleasure.

As you can see, we have a lively batch of stories, delivering the very best in page-turning romance. Happy reading!

Sincerely,

Karen Taylor Richman
Senior Editor

Please address questions and book requests to:
Silhouette Reader Service
U.S.: 3010 Walden Ave., P.O. Box 1325, Buffalo, NY 14269
Canadian: P.O. Box 609, Fort Erie, Ont. L2A 5X3

Balancing Act

LILIAN DARCY

SPECIAL EDITION™

Published by Silhouette Books

America's Publisher of Contemporary Romance

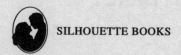 SILHOUETTE BOOKS

ISBN 0-373-24552-1

BALANCING ACT

Copyright © 2003 by Melissa Benyon

This edition published by arrangement with Harlequin Books S.A.

Visit Silhouette at www.eHarlequin.com

Printed in U.S.A.

LILIAN DARCY

has written over fifty books for Silhouette Romance and Harlequin Mills & Boon Medical Romance (Prescription Romance). Her first book for Silhouette appeared on the Waldenbooks Series Romance Bestsellers list, and she's hoping readers go on responding strongly to her work. Happily married with four active children and a very patient cat, she enjoys keeping busy and could probably fill several more lifetimes with the things she likes to do—including cooking, gardening, quilting, drawing and traveling. She currently lives in Australia but travels to the United States as often as possible to visit family. Lilian loves to hear from readers. You can write to her at P.O. Box 381, Hackensack, NJ 07602 or e-mail her at lildarcy@austarmetro.com.au.

Dear Reader,

This was always a special book for me, and I was so pleased when it was scheduled as my first Special Edition novel. Libby and Brady really needed a long book with a rich emotional tone to tell their story fully.

The week after my editor phoned with the news, I flew from Australia to Denver to attend the Romance Writers of America annual conference. On the flight from San Francisco to Denver there were four darling little Korean babies going to their new adoptive homes in the U.S. and this seemed like a perfect omen for *Balancing Act*. One of the flight attendants and I stood at the back of the plane for half the flight, holding two of the babies. They were smiling and bright-eyed and totally adorable. We got quite teary thinking of the long journey they were making to their new life and their new parents. It was easy to believe that there was something magical and predestined about the whole thing.

As you'll see when you read *Balancing Act*, Libby and Brady embrace their destiny when they realize that the two babies they've independently adopted are identical twins. It's not an easy journey for them, but when the happiness of their daughters is at stake, there's no choice.

I really hope you enjoy this book.

Lilian Darcy

Chapter One

Brady Buchanan would be here with his little daughter in twenty minutes, maybe less. Libby McGraw hadn't even heard of the man four days ago, but already, without yet having met him, she had the strongest intuition that he was going to be an important figure in her life.

"If I hadn't entered Colleen in the Bright and Beautiful baby contest," she muttered to herself, "I might never have known…"

A part of her regretted that contest bitterly now, although she'd been so pleased and proud and excited when Colleen had won and had been photographed for the magazine, "with proud mother Lisa-Belle McGraw, of Minnesota."

Libby tried to focus on something—*anything*—but she couldn't. There was a nagging, crampy ache low in her stomach and she knew it was only partly phys-

ical. Circling back to the bathroom mirror for the
third time, she fussed with her appearance a little
more. She pulled the clips out of her hair, then
combed it, twisted it up and put the clips back in.

No, she decided. Leave it down.

Out came the clips again. Up went the brush to
put in some shine. Yes, her hair definitely looked
better framing her face today. Softer. And it cam-
ouflaged the fact that she looked so stressed-out and
tired.

She reapplied her lip gloss in a brighter shade, then
wondered if it, too, left her skin looking too white.
She tended to lose color when she was stressed.
Since Monday, she'd gone through her makeup at
twice the normal rate and had slept about half the
hours she needed.

She heard a sound, listened in case it was Colleen
and, creeping into her daughter's room, found her
still napping. The dark, silky hair around her temples
was a little damp, as if she was hot. Libby was hot,
too. She felt as if she was burning up.

It was just after four in the afternoon. Friday afternoon. He—Brady Buchanan—had said that his
flight was getting in at quarter to three. He had to
pick up his rental car, then check himself and his
daughter into their motel. It was one of the motels
right opposite the Mall of America, just across In-
terstate 494, which ran along beside the airport.

When he'd checked in, he was coming right over.
The drive across the river into St. Paul would take
him around fifteen minutes. Maybe a little more if
there was traffic.

And then he would be here, with a little girl named
Scarlett.

Libby still hoped against hope that it would all turn out to be a huge mistake. She'd entered Colleen in the baby contest and Colleen had won. Brady had seen Colleen's picture on the front page of the parenting magazine which had sponsored the contest, and she appeared—*appeared*—identical to his own little girl.

Twins, like two peas in a pod.

Since they'd each adopted their mixed-race daughters from the same orphanage in Vietnam, it wasn't as impossible as it sounded.

Face-to-face, however, it would turn out that their girls wouldn't look alike at all, and this overwhelming situation would be over before it had properly begun. She hoped so, desperately, fervently, blindly, because if not...

Libby was terrified about the whole thing, terrified about what Brady Buchanan would want, and what kind of a man he would be. Her instinct was to be deeply wary about the potential complications involved, and about how vulnerable she might become.

Four days ago, on the phone, out of the blue, she hadn't had the slightest idea what the man was talking about at first. She'd been on the verge of concluding that it was a prank call, or worse. Some creep had gotten enough detail from the story in *Parenting Now* to find her in the St. Paul telephone directory.

But then Mr. Buchanan had changed tack suddenly. His voice—deep, with a slightly roughened note in it, like fine sandpaper sliding across heavy wood—had softened.

"Okay, you're not getting this, are you?" he'd said. "Or you don't believe me, I guess. Which I can understand. But it's true. It has to be."

"*What's* true?"

"Remember the orphanage?"

"How did you know—" She'd stopped abruptly, afraid of what she might be giving away. She'd learned a deep reliance on privacy and self-sufficiency during her adult years, and was very careful to whom she told the details of how she'd gotten her darling baby, despite the fact that the adoption was in full compliance with international law.

But then something about Brady Buchanan's voice compelled her to listen as he went on with those evocative questions, his words a little clumsy in their emotion, his phrases disjointed and stumbling over themselves.

"Did you see the white cotton diapers, the way they had 'em spread out to dry on the bushes?" he'd said. "And remember the heat? And did all the local people, when you were in Da Nang, when you went out into the streets with the baby, did they crowd around you, smiling and asking questions?"

"So you're saying—"

"Did you see the sand at My Khe beach, how it was so white? And did you taste that fantastic seafood? That's where you got your daughter from, isn't it? From the orphanage outside of Da Nang?"

"Yes. Yes, I did," she'd answered him shakily. "That's where my daughter came from, too."

"Oh, mercy, it's not possible!"

"Ms. McGraw, it has to be!"

They'd talked about it for nearly twenty minutes, arranging a way to meet as soon as he could get away from his work, trying to piece together the girls' story. All of it was conjecture, most of it coming from him, since he'd had longer to think about it.

What would he be like? And what would he want to do if their girls really were twins? She'd been tossing the options back and forth in her mind for four days and four sleepless nights. There weren't many of those options, and each of them had huge ramifications.

Oh criminy, she was terrified!

Two things cut across her darting thoughts. First, she heard Colleen, who had woken from her nap in tears, as she often did. Then, as she went to pick up her crying daughter, Libby heard the doorbell ring and knew it would be him.

Brady Buchanan.

The man who owned that dark, husky, emotional voice.

The man who was adoptive father to the child who could be—*could* be—her daughter's twin.

"In a minute," she called, and hurried into Colleen's room. He could probably hear her crying, even from the porch.

Colleen was standing in her crib, face screwed up, mouth open wide and tears pouring down her cheeks. Libby lifted her up and began to soothe her as she headed down the stairs. By the time she had reached the front door, Colleen was quiet. Normally, she cried for longer when she woke late like this. Had she sensed that something important was about to happen?

Libby took a deep breath and opened the door, praying yet again that Brady Buchanan would be wrong. This wouldn't be important at all.

He wasn't wrong.

She knew it the moment she saw her daughter—*her daughter!*—in the arms of a total stranger. No, *not* her daughter, despite that instinctive moment of possessiveness and panic and leaping emotion.

This was Colleen's sister. Her twin sister.

On the phone, Brady had talked about blood tests, and Libby had agreed. Now, she already knew that the tests would be purely a formality. The girls were identical. Silky hair, curious eyes, neat little shoulders, fine-drawn mouths.

Identical, except for the way they were dressed. In place of Colleen's matched set of lilac floral, lace-edged T-shirt and pants, Scarlett Buchanan was dressed in a red-and-gray stretch playsuit emblazoned across the front with the words Born To Be a Buckeye. It looked as if her dad was a college football fan and a graduate of Ohio State.

Scarlett's dad…

Libby looked at him for the first time. Only a few seconds had passed since she'd pushed open the door but it felt like much longer, and neither of them had yet spoken a word. She still couldn't, because there was some kind of invisible hand clamped right across her throat. Instead, she just looked at him standing there—a little awkward, possibly as terrified as she was—with her daughter's twin propped on his arm.

He wasn't a huge man. Slightly above average height, that was all. Five-eleven, say. But he was solid as a rock. Chest like a brick wall. Shoulders padded with muscle. Washboard abs, without a doubt, beneath his clothing. You couldn't have scraped enough fat off his frame to grease a muffin pan.

He had a few threads of premature silver in his light-brown hair, which was cut short and practical, and the faintest reddish-brown shadow of new growth on his jaw. As she gaped helplessly at him, he scraped his hand across it and she heard the light friction of callused palms against stubble.

His skin had some living in it. It was outdoor skin, tanned but not moisturized, clean but not pampered. She remembered he'd told her, over the phone, that he owned and operated his own construction company, which probably accounted for that rugged look. It also accounted for why he hadn't been able to get here until today.

Both of them had wanted to hop straight on a plane, but he'd had project commitments he couldn't break, and Colleen had been getting over an ear infection, so Libby was reluctant to fly.

"Hi," he said. His smile was careful, brief.

And his eyes were blue. Complex blue. The kind that looked gray in some lights and deep, smoky green in others. On the tail end of the half smile, he frowned, and those changeable eyes seemed to darken. For a fleeting moment, Libby wondered how they would look in bright sunshine when he was laughing. Say, when he was watching his football team win their game.

He was wearing an Ohio State Buckeyes sweatshirt—gray with scarlet lettering, over newish blue jeans. The clothing showed off the breadth of his shoulders and the lean strength of his thighs. She'd met bigger men and stronger men, but there was something about the potent aura of maleness surrounding Brady Buchanan that affected her powerfully. She felt as though someone had picked up a big wooden spoon and started stirring it around deep in her crampy, aching stomach.

Was it only because she was so terrified about how

much potential he had to change her life? *Ruin* her life? She'd faced that fear in the dark hours of every night since his call. She'd even wondered whether she would have reacted in the same confident way that he had if she had been the one to see a photo of her daughter's twin in a magazine.

Would she have called every Buchanan in Ohio until she'd reached him? Or would she have convinced herself that it wasn't possible, it had to be a mistake, and let her contented, self-reliant life go on just as it was?

It would have been very easy to play it that way. "Accidentally" lose the magazine and forget his last name. Convince herself that the girls only looked alike because of the angle of the photo. Tell herself that the adoption authorities would surely have known if there was a twin sister, so she had to be mistaken.

Brady hadn't used any of those excuses to opt out. He'd taken the morally right and decisive action at once. He'd accessed all of Minnesota's telephone directories via the Internet, had kept calling until he'd found her, and now, here he was.

What would she do if they disliked each other within five minutes? If his ideas on how to deal with this situation were impossibly different from hers? And what would *he* do?

Strong men could get in the habit of winning, of dominating with their decisions, and it was a hard habit to break. Immediately, she didn't trust the way he had his feet planted so squarely on her porch, or the way his jaw and mouth had set. He looked too much like a man who believed in simple solutions.

His solutions. She didn't want that kind of man in her life again.

Stop this, she coached herself angrily. Don't leap to conclusions. Get a grip. Listen to him. Communicate. Don't duck the issues. Stand your ground. And right now, *say* something.

"Please come in," said Lisa-Belle McGraw at last, her voice sweet and polite. They hadn't been standing here in the doorway all that long. Maybe half a minute. But it seemed like half of forever.

She looked even more nervous than Brady felt. That was saying something, since he felt as though his tie was choking him and he wasn't even wearing one. She held her daughter's soft dark curls against her cheek in a gesture of tender possession, unconsciously emphasizing the contrast in their coloring.

Brady had expected they'd need to sit the two girls down side by side in order to compare them properly and turn their suspicions into certainty. Maybe even dress them in similar outfits or something, in order to decide whether to go ahead with the blood tests. But already it wasn't necessary, and blood tests would only be the icing on the cake.

Just the way Colleen moved, the expression on her face, everything about her except her clothes, was so identical to Scarlett. He could tell that she'd woken from her late nap in tears, because that was what Scarlett always did, and that was how she always looked when it happened. Red and crumpled, sad and irritable.

He knew that even though Colleen had stopped crying, she would look a little zoned-out for several more minutes, and she would cling to whoever was holding her and occasionally turn to bury her face in their shoulder.

Yep, there she goes...

It was uncanny to feel as if he already knew this little girl. It tugged painfully on his heart. He remembered how he and Stacey had both bonded instantly with Scarlett, the first moment she was laid in Stacey's arms.

"This your baby," the orphanage worker had told them, in her broken English, and they'd loved their little girl from that moment on. How could Brady meet her twin sister and not start to feel the same?

His heart lurched again. Sideways. Out of balance.

Shift over in there, Scarlett, and make room. You don't have the place to yourself anymore. There's someone else I need to love now.

Someone who already had a family of her own and a life here in St. Paul.

How on earth would they deal with this?

Scarlett had napped early, and she was bright as a button in his arms right now—curious and happy and ready to toddle off at breakneck speed and explore. Ms. McGraw knew all about that, Brady could tell. Just as he knew her child, this stranger knew his little daughter. Was her heart lurching sideways, too?

After another intense look at Scarlett, she scraped her teeth over her bottom lip and repeated, even more nervously, "Please, you really must come in!"

She reached out, pushing the storm door open a little wider. The movement tightened the light fabric of a pink-and-blue summery top across her breasts. She had a neat figure, petite and curved just right, enough to give a man something to hold, and something to watch when she walked.

Brady stepped forward and suddenly he caught her scent for the first time. It reached out and drew him in, and his stride and his breathing both faltered as he walked quickly past her, still caught in its sweet net. It was like lilacs after rain, cool and intoxicating. It was like…

No. *No!*

He wasn't a poetic man. It wasn't like lilacs and rain at all. It was a punch in the gut that almost knocked him off his feet. It was a trip wire stretched across his path. Responding to Lisa-Belle McGraw as a man was the last thing in the world he'd expected or wanted. Primitive. Beyond logic or personality. And potentially disastrous.

He'd been there before, with Stacey, when he was too young to know any better—going crazy for her body and never stopping to find out who she really was. Finding out had cooled the craziness as time went on, but by then it was too late. Brady wasn't going to make the same mistake again.

It was vital to keep his head clear here. He had something else to think about. Something much more vital to his emotional well-being than the physical tricks a female body could play. And apparently Ms. McGraw had her eye on the ball much better than he did.

"If people see us and get an inkling as to what's going on…" she was saying behind him. "I don't want to have to tell anyone about this yet. Not until we've worked out what it means. I—I have an idea it's going to be, uh, pretty big."

"Yeah, you're right," he agreed, his voice gruff and deep, and went ahead of her into the house, out of reach of the aura that had briefly ensnared him.

As he responded to Scarlett's wriggling and put her onto her feet, first impressions piled into his mind. Ms. McGraw had a nice house on a street just two blocks south of the Minnesota governor's mansion. He'd already noted the quiet prosperity of the neighborhood as he drove here. It was similar to the neighborhood he'd bought into in Columbus several years ago, when his construction business really took off.

The interior of the house was immaculate, furnished in florals and pastels, with a thick cream rug covering most of the hardwood floor. Photos and knickknacks were everywhere: decorative plates on the dusky-pink walls, and fresh flowers in vases on the old-fashioned piano as well as on the dining table he glimpsed in the next room. It was a real home, reflecting one caring woman's taste. It wasn't a place you'd easily uproot from.

And Lisa-Belle McGraw looked as if she belonged. She was a natural Minnesota blond princess, with hair that reminded him of that fairy tale, "Rumpelstiltskin," about the goblin with the unique name who had known how to spin straw into gold. He could easily have been practising his talent on this woman's hair. Silky, straw-colored strands, as straight as a waterfall, mingled with shiny threads that looked like pure gold in the last of the day's September sunlight slanting through her living-room windows.

She was too pale, even with makeup, and it made both her eyes and her lips stand out. Eyes like a tropical ocean, lips that glistened like candy melting in the heat. She'd dressed up for this meeting, he guessed, as he took in her strappy pumps and the pastel swirl of feminine fabric that clung to her body.

She was as pretty as he'd seen in her photo in *Parenting Now*. Actually, she was more than pretty. Definitely not something he wanted to be so aware of, he reminded himself. He wasn't in the market for a new relationship any time soon, and certainly not with this woman. Even if he liked the way she smelled.

He needed to move farther away from the memories of his marriage first.

His heart sank as he considered the possibility of emotional scenes, energy-sapping manipulation, hidden motives and downright dishonesty. In a situation like this, those things might easily happen if he didn't play everything right. He'd had more than enough of all that with Stacey, and though he'd grieved for her in a complicated, upside-down kind of way, he couldn't help doubting that they would have stayed the distance, had she lived. By the end, she'd lied to him a few times too often.

"Do you want to come out back, where they can play?"

Ms. McGraw's question dragged his focus back to where it ought to have been all along. Scarlett was toddling around the living room, eager to explore. Colleen watched her from the safety of her mother's arms.

"I expect Scarlett would like that," he said.

"We can sit on the deck and have some coffee while we watch them." She clasped her hands briefly, then brushed a stray silk ribbon of hair away from her face. "I—this is such a weird situation. I'm sorry, I don't know where to begin or what to suggest.''

''Coffee sounds good,'' he answered gruffly.

Coffee was the tip of the iceberg. It was the next twenty years that occupied both their minds.

''If you want to wash up first...?'' she offered, her politeness apparently ingrained and automatic. Once again, her voice was sweet and clear.

''Yeah. Thanks.''

She indicated a little powder room tucked away beneath the stairs, and he barged into it, needing a few moments alone, and hoping that cool water streaming over his hands would cool his whole body down.

The exercise wasn't a success. For a start, Scarlett got clingy and stood outside the door, crying persistently. He heard that sweet female voice again, inviting her to go out back and try the slide, but Scarlett wasn't having any of that. No instant, instinctive bonding for her, thank you very much. She was too young to recognize the mirrorlike familiarity of that other little girl, and eighteen months was a clingy age. Brady wanted to hurry back out to her, which made him even clumsier than he'd already felt.

Ms. McGraw had maddening soaps—tiny pastel-toned seashell shapes, nestling in a glass dish. His big hands knocked several of them out onto the pristine vanity unit, and when he'd finally grabbed one, his wet palms sent it spurting out of his fingers. It ricocheted off the door, hit the bud vase on the windowsill and knocked it over. An apricot-hued rose fell to the floor.

Brady had never liked fussy decor, and now he

knew why. If Ms. McGraw had heard the soap hitting the door and the vase hitting the sill, she probably wondered what on earth he was doing in here.

And Scarlett was still crying. Louder than ever. He could hear her little hands, batting at the door.

At least nothing was broken. He pressed his hands together, across his nose and mouth, and blew a long breath through his fingers, then studied his image in the mirror. He wasn't happy about what he saw.

For a start, he should have shaved again at the motel. He looked like a thug. His jaw had felt as rough as a metal rasp just now beneath his tension-knotted hands.

And he was too casually dressed. He should have worn a buttoned-down shirt and a jacket. Like this, with his gut still churning, he felt that he didn't project enough authority or enough intellect. He might need both those qualities, if he and this woman disagreed, at a fundamental level, about what they needed to do.

In the brains department, he wasn't a pushover. He had a college degree, and the construction company he owned was tendering for bigger and more important jobs every year and getting them. He'd never doubted himself in that area. But he wasn't great with words, and emotional scenes tied his tongue in knots.

There were some emotional scenes coming up. There had to be! They had the futures of two little girls weighing in the balance, and they lived in cities that were more than seven hundred miles apart.

What if Lisa-Belle McGraw expected him to make all the sacrifices? What if she had a plan for getting what she wanted, and he didn't see it coming until it was too late?

Scarlett wailed louder, and he told her, ''I'm still here, baby. I'll be out in two seconds.''

He bent to pick up the fallen rose, stuck it roughly back in the vase and filled the little glass tube with fresh water. It overflowed and saturated his hands, as well as an inch of one sleeve. With Scarlett still crying outside, he left without taking time to use the towel, and had to dry his hands on the back of his pants before scooping his little girl into his arms once more.

Passing through the spotless kitchen and onto the wooden rear deck, he found his daughter's twin sister's mother already there with two porcelain mugs of coffee on a tray, some milk in sippy cups for the girls, and a plate of dainty cookies arranged on a paper lace doily.

Their cue for some polite, meaningless conversation?

Not on Ms. McGraw's agenda, apparently. He was surprised at the determined look which had appeared on her pretty face, but it gave him a brief warning of her intentions and left him a little better prepared. Almost relieved, too. Whatever she wanted, he would much prefer it if she went after it openly and honestly, if she said what was on her mind so that they both knew where they stood.

''I don't want to pursue this through official channels,'' she said. Her voice started out wobbly and ended up firm.

''Pursue what?'' he asked, betraying his impatience, and his ill ease. ''The question of whether the girls are twins? Isn't it obvious, after one glance, that

they are? The blood tests are only going to con-
firm it.''

"Yes, it's—'' she took a deep breath, and tried to
smile ''—uncannily obvious.'' The smile wobbled
and fell off her face, like a loose wheel falling off a
toy cart. "I never imagined that they could look so
much alike, even when I considered that you might
be right. When I first saw your daughter, I wanted to
snatch her right out of your arms.'' Her voice
dropped to a husky whisper.

"I know the feeling,'' he drawled.

She pulled herself together, and her voice firmed.
"No, I just meant that I don't want to tell anyone
about it. Not Immigration or the adoption people.''

"I don't think it would invalidate the adoptions,
Ms. McGraw. I can't see how it could.''

"Please, call me Libby.''

"Okay. Libby.'' He tried it out on his tongue, but
couldn't decide if he liked it. On the one hand, it was
a snappy little nickname, and an inventive way to
contract the more formal Lisa-Belle. On the other, it
was a little too cute. He wasn't big on cute.

"I guess I'm just not prepared to take any kind of
a chance on the adoptions,'' she said. The fall air
was crisp and cool, and she shivered a little as she
spoke. On the grass in her yard, there was already a
carpet of fallen yellow leaves. "If there was ever any
risk that I might lose Colleen...''

"No one's talking about either of us losing our
daughters.'' The very thought opened a pit of fear in
his gut. "The adoptions were both done in full ac-
cordance with the...you know, you must have read
the information about it...the Hague Convention on
Intercountry Adoption,'' he reminded her. "You

know how strict Vietnam is on that issue, and the United States, too. Stacey and I wouldn't have gotten involved with the idea if there'd been anything dodgy about it.''

"Me, neither.'' She paused, then added gently, "I'm sorry, it must have been hard for you to lose your wife so soon after you'd both become parents at last.''

He nodded, and muttered something. He'd told her over the phone that he was widowed, that his wife's death had been sudden and unexpected, the result of an accident. What he hadn't told her was that the blood alcohol level of the man Stacey had been driving with—her lover—had been well over the legal limit at the time.

It wasn't a piece of information he enjoyed sharing with strangers, and he definitely didn't want this woman asking questions about the state of his marriage. If that led to any kind of doubt over his capability as a father...

Would he and Libby be able to remain strangers, though?

Looking covertly at her, he wondered about how she was situated. She'd lost her husband more than four years ago. Enough time to grieve, and for the memories to soften. In the dating department, she couldn't be short of offers if she wanted them. Not a pretty woman like her, a woman who smelled like flowers and rain and springtime. Was there anyone else in her life whom he needed to consider?

And in Scarlett's? What kind of a connection were they making this weekend? How should he respond to that immediate impulse to take Scarlett's twin into his heart?

Shift over, Scarlett.

He knew he could love two daughters without being unfair to either of them. The girls could build a precious bond with each other, and his mom would adore another grandchild. But where did Lisa-Belle McGraw fit in?

"So what do you want to do?" he asked her. Despite the colorless phrasing, they both understood what an enormous question it was.

"Talk a little more, first, about what might have happened," she answered, her voice still firm. "I need to get the dates straight. I just need to understand the history." She pressed her fingertips to her temples. "You and your wife took Scarlett from the orphanage, when, exactly?"

"June twelfth." He had the date down pat, like a birthday or an anniversary. Scarlett's exact birth date wasn't known. "Fifteen months ago."

"I was there around ten weeks later. August twentieth. I was told Colleen had just been left on the veranda at night. Someone heard her cry at around midnight and went out and found her. No idea about either of her parents, except that her father, most likely, was white and her mother was probably mixed race. I'm thinking the mom would have been conceived back during the war..."

"Yes, in the sixties or early seventies."

"...with an American GI father. But all of that's just conjecture, based on the way she looks. The way *they* look," she corrected herself quickly.

"We were told pretty much the same story," Brady answered. "Whether the orphanage workers had any inkling the girls were sisters... Probably not, since they passed through the place at different times.

I got the impression the orphanage gets its share of mixed-race babies.''

"Yes, so did I.''

"I'm guessing the mother kept one baby in the hope she could manage to raise it, then found after a couple of months that she couldn't.''

"I can't imagine what that must have been like for her. I try not to think about it. Maybe she felt better knowing that her baby would be going to a better life.''

"That's what we told ourselves, also.''

"It was for the best, I'm sure of it.''

"And of course," he went on, "by the time she brought Colleen in, the orphanage would have had other kids passing through, and staff coming and going, possibly. And anyhow, a baby changes so much in those first few months.''

"I guess that's how it happened,'' she agreed. "And that's where I'm happy to leave it. Whatever the exact story is, it doesn't change what we're facing now.''

"No, I guess it doesn't.''

Brady took a sip of his coffee, debating on whether to reach for a cookie as well. They looked melt-in-the-mouth good, but the way they were arranged on that doily made them seem as if they were only for show. He'd already ruined Lisa-Belle's little soap arrangement in the powder room. Didn't want to do the same with the cookies.

Instead of taking one, he dampened down his hunger and watched the girls. Scarlett had discovered the sturdy plastic slide and playhouse set, and was exploring its ins and outs. Colleen came down the little slide. Showing off, maybe, or staking out her territory? More likely, at eighteen months, she was just having fun.

She tipped back too far on the way down, bumped hard onto her bottom and scrambled to her feet, taking the rough landing in stride just as Scarlett always did. Next time Colleen came down, Scarlett was right behind her, and both of them were laughing. They were active, vital little girls.

"The only thing I know for sure, right now, is that it would be wrong for them to grow up not knowing each other, not having the chance to be sisters," Brady said, his voice suddenly husky. "And for me, too. How could I love one little girl and not the other? It would just be *wrong*."

Shoot!

He hadn't planned to say it. The words had just *happened*, falling out of his mouth, blunt as always, as soon as they crystallized in his thoughts. He looked across to where Libby McGraw sat, in a cedarwood outdoor chair just like the one he was sitting in.

Her legs were crossed at her ankles and her hands were clasped around her knees, neat and pretty and careful. Hell, and his heart was beating so much harder and faster as he waited for her reply that he could actually feel it thumping inside his chest.

Why was he so scared about what he'd given away? Why was he *instantly* sorry he'd laid his beliefs on the table like that?

Because he'd intended to find out what *she* thought and felt first.

With unsteady hands, he took two of the cookies at once and ate them in a single bite. They tasted like Christmas morning when he was eight years old.

"Why would it be wrong, Brady?" she asked carefully, after a long pause.

It wasn't the tack he had expected her to take. He was relieved about that, but still very suspicious, on shifting ground. Something didn't ring true in what she'd just said. "Don't you agree?" he asked her.

"There are plenty of kids that grow up as only children, these days," she answered. Her chin was raised and her eyes were too bright.

"True, but—"

"I wouldn't have adopted Colleen in the first place if I'd thought I couldn't meet all of her needs," she went on, gathering speed. "I refinanced my home and took a pay cut so I could work at a high-quality day-care center and have her there with me."

"I'm not saying—"

"I used to teach kindergarten, but that wouldn't have given us the time with each other that I wanted. She gets plenty of social interaction at day care with kids her own age. If I hadn't entered her in that contest, she and Scarlett could have gone their whole lives not knowing about each other, and they'd still have been loved and nourished and happy. They'd have missed nothing."

Her voice was high and sweet and very firm.

Too firm.

Her eyes, in contrast, were frightened and defiant.

Okay, he understood, now.

"You don't believe a single word of what you're saying," Brady growled at her, and sure enough, she flashed him a startled look and her cheeks went bright pink. "You *don't*," he repeated.

There was a silence.

"Yeah, okay, you're right," she agreed quietly at

last. Her clasped hands had tightened around her knees, and her shoulders were rounded, vulnerable looking. There was anguish in her face now. "You're right. I don't."

She shook her head, and the tiny silver earrings that were nestled against her pink lobes flashed.

"You know," she went on, "I've been saying it to myself every minute since your call on Monday. I've tried to make myself believe it doesn't make a difference, but I can't." Brady could see how hard she found it to put her emotions into words. "We have to give them the chance to be sisters, don't we? And we have to give ourselves the chance to love both of them. But you're in Ohio and I'm in Minnesota, and I can't begin to think about how we're going to do it. It—it might have been easier if we'd never known."

"I know," he answered, then confessed abruptly, "All the way here on the airplane, I was wishing my mom had never seen that magazine."

Chapter Two

"I can stay until Sunday," Brady said. "We can think about it. There are options. You know, a lot of people manage shared custody of their kids after a divorce, even when they're living in different states. People manage to have their kids visit far-away grandparents. It's not insurmountable."

"No, I guess it isn't," Libby answered obediently. She popped a little smile onto her face, then added, "More coffee?" and when he nodded and said, "Please!" it gave her an excuse to go into the house, where she could rebel in private.

She didn't want Brady to see how much his words about managing "shared custody" had terrified her. One look at that little girl in his arms, identical to her own Colleen, had told her how easily she could come to love two daughters, but how could she share two daughters with a stranger?

Did he expect her just to hand Colleen over for weekends and vacation visits? Put her on a plane and send her seven hundred miles? Dear Lord, no!

Her own parents had divorced when she was eight, and she'd had to do that. Just step on a plane every few months. The memories weren't good, and she didn't revisit them very often. Mom had never really adjusted to the divorce and to being a single parent. She hadn't been prepared for managing on her own, so they'd moved from Kansas City to Chicago to be closer to Libby's grandparents, and it had taken Mom a long time to find her feet.

She'd been horrified when Libby had taken on the role of single mother voluntarily. "If Glenn was still alive of course I'd have loved a grandchild, but not like this, Libby. You don't know how hard it's going to be."

But Libby had cherished her independence and her freedom to run her life the way she chose. She hadn't had that same freedom in her marriage. And now Brady was talking about "shared custody" as if it was easy and safe, as if it was something they could both just slot into their lives. He had no idea!

I should have challenged him on it. But maybe if I work as hard as I can to make this weekend nice and fun and harmonious, we can talk on Sunday and we'll find there is *another answer.*

Even as she thought this, she knew it was a cop-out on her part. The kind of cop-out she'd made before, and didn't want to make again. But wanting something and achieving it were two very different things, she'd found, especially when life came at you sideways like a runaway train.

Still unsure of how she would handle the situation,

she poured two fresh mugs of coffee and went back out to the rear deck. Brady had vanished from the deck chair, and a few seconds of panicky searching—he was a stranger, she knew almost nothing about him, and she'd left him with her precious daughter, was she crazy?—revealed him safely down in the yard with the girls.

Oh, mercy, what a sight it was!

Silently, she put the coffee mugs down on the barbecue table and watched. Somehow, he'd gotten himself horizontal on the damp grass, solid as a fallen log, and both girls were running to and fro, covering him deeply with leaves.

They were shrieking with laughter—*identical* laughter—tossing wild handfuls of color every which way and earning exaggerated protests from Brady which they clearly found hilarious.

"More leaves? We're having *more* leaves?" he was saying in that gravelly voice she was starting to know. "What? I'm not buried deep enough for you, yet, guys? I swear—"

Then he caught sight of Libby and stopped abruptly, and she had to hide a laugh of her own at the sight of his face.

He was *blushing?*

No, it had to be the effort and exertion of all that protesting, followed by the sudden scramble to his feet.

"I...uh..." he said, and brushed himself down, strong shoulders moving beneath the gray fabric of his sweatshirt. "That was...you know..."

"I know," she answered, still laughing. "They loved it."

She wanted him to laugh with her, but he'd closed

off, retreated somehow. Coming up the steps and reaching for the coffee mug she still held in her hand, he looked intimidating and serious, a construction company boss through and through, not the kind of man you'd ever catch horsing around with two little girls.

Libby was sorry, now, that she'd caught him out. She didn't want to create more distance than necessary.

Their fingers touched briefly as he took the mug. As a piece of body contact, it was nothing. Quicker and lighter than the touch of a makeup brush on her cheek, or the flick of her hand when she shooed a mosquito from Colleen's face. All the same, it was warm and physical and potent, and she wished it hadn't happened.

Possibly he did, too.

If he'd even noticed it, Libby revised. She doubted that the imprint of it had lingered on his skin the way it was still lingering on hers. And she doubted that her scent was still wrapping around him, the way his had wrapped around her. It was clean and male, reminding her of freshly shaven wood, and it was mixed with the earthy scent of the leaves.

He could have had half a dozen better reasons for moving away from her so quickly, with that distant frown still on his face.

Brady knew he was frowning too much, knew it made him look distant—intimidating, even—and he didn't care. Deliberately, he turned his back on Libby, took a big mouthful of coffee and stared down at the fall color carpeting the yard.

He shouldn't have fooled around with the leaves

like that. He couldn't afford to have this woman think he was soft, lacking intelligence, easy to manipulate, easy to distract from his goals with a bit of pretty color, and ready to take care of everything as needed.

Even though he *was* soft. He knew that. When it came to Scarlett's well-being, he was a pussycat. He turned to liquid inside, like a soft-centered chocolate candy, every time he felt her little arms around his neck, or saw her smile, or had to kiss a bump.

And when it came to Scarlett, he *would* take care of everything as needed. He would walk over hot coals to give her the things she should have. A play in the leaves. Pretty toys at Christmas. A college education. Her very own twin sister.

What kind of sacrifices was Libby McGraw prepared to make? he wondered.

They drank their coffee mostly in silence, just watching the girls and commenting occasionally on their play. Inwardly, Libby was working on her courage, putting it in place piece by piece, like building a solid brick wall.

She waited until Brady had drained his mug, then cleared her throat—it shouldn't have been so tight, but it was—and said, "How about we go out for pizza? There's a place just a few blocks from here that's kid-friendly, and the girls should stay the distance, don't you think, after their naps? It's not even six, yet. Seven, Ohio time."

"Shouldn't be a problem," he agreed.

She took a deep breath and forced herself to speak. "Because I don't want to leave it until the end of the weekend before we talk about this, Brady. I want to get it on the table tonight, so that we both know where we stand.''

He looked at her, and she could see the speculation and assessment in his face. He didn't fully trust her. It was written in the jut of his jaw and the narrowing of his eyes. It was shouted by the frequent glances he gave toward both the girls. Definitely, he didn't trust her.

The feeling was mutual, and maybe that was good. Staying on her guard was a lot better than the alternatives.

Since it was still pretty early, they had their pick of several tables at the pizza restaurant, and chose one in a quiet corner in back, near the open kitchen. The girls were happy to squiggle with crayons on sheets of paper, watch the pizzas sliding in and out of the big, wood-fired oven and slurp their juice.

''Have you always lived in St. Paul?'' Brady asked Libby as they waited for their order, and she couldn't help her suspicion that it was more than just a casual question. Had she once again lost the initiative she was seeking?

''No, I was born in Kansas City,'' she answered him, too accustomed to behaving as good manners dictated. She wasn't prepared to avoid his question, or to challenge it, no matter how suspicious of it she was. ''But I grew up in Chicago after my parents got divorced. I met my husband at Northwestern—he was doing his master's—and we moved here when his company transferred him, around ten years ago, right after I finished college.''

''You've moved around some, then. I was born in Columbus, and I've stayed there.''

"So Scarlett is a third-generation Buckeye fan?"

He laughed. It was the kind of laugh that invited a response, deep and chuckling, like a little stream gurgling way down in a forest's secret hollows. "Fifth."

"Wow!"

"My grandfather used to take me to games when I was a kid, and his father took him. I've been taking Scarlett since she was a baby. Not sure how she'll go this season, now that she wants to run around."

"That's nice."

His eyes were nice, too. Libby didn't want to notice the fact, but it was a little hard not to, when they were looking at her from just a few feet away, across the table. She was right in what she'd seen earlier. They didn't always look blue. Now, for instance, you'd have said they were gray—dark and smoky and thoughtful.

She got the impression he wasn't an intellectual man—not the kind of person who read serious books and watched documentaries on TV—but he wasn't stupid, either. He was the kind of person who kept his thought processes to himself, then came out with surprising results in the end. Take his next question, for example.

"Were you and your husband trying to have a baby for long?" he asked. "Were you on that whole assisted reproduction treadmill, like Stacey and I put ourselves through?"

"No, we hadn't been trying long at all," she answered, startled into honesty. A couple's fertility wasn't something most people wanted to ask about at a first meeting. As it happened, she and Glenn hadn't had time to discover whether they had any problems in that area. "Just three or four months," she added. "Glenn hadn't felt ready until he hit thirty-seven."

Too late, she realized what she'd unconsciously implied—that she herself had been ready much sooner.

Well, that was true, wasn't it? Although ten years younger than he was, she'd been ready for a long time, but Glenn had stood firm, as always. He wasn't ready to share her with a baby yet. He wanted her all to himself. He still had career goals to accomplish. He didn't want to be tied down and woken in the night. She had pretended to herself for years that she understood those reasons, and that she didn't mind.

She just wished she hadn't let Brady Buchanan in on the secret. There had been some dissatisfactions in her marriage before Glenn's illness. For the sake of the deeper connection they'd made with each other during those last months when Glenn had softened so much, however, she kept those to herself.

It seemed weird to be talking on such a personal level with Brady, a near-stranger, but discovering that you shared twin daughters with a man cut through some of the usual barriers.

Some of them.

In other areas, she felt even more wary, and more protective of secrets and doubts and resolutions.

She went on quickly, "Then his cancer was diagnosed, and that was the end of it. With the type of cancer and treatment he had, there was no possibility of getting another chance to conceive once his treatment was over, even if he had survived."

"That must have been tough."

"It was. A double loss, in a lot of ways. My hus-

band, and my chance for a child that was his. Even
so, it took me a long time to decide on adoption. I
knew it would be a major undertaking on my own.''

"Stacey and I tried to have a baby for eight
years," Brady said. "Deciding to go for an intercountry adoption gave us the best year of our marriage.''

It didn't quite make sense. They'd only had Scarlett for two or three months before his wife's death.
He must have been including the months before that.

Libby couldn't agree on those months being good
ones in her own case. Although she'd appreciated the
need for all the bureaucratic red tape in two coun-
tries, in order to ensure that children were willingly
given up to responsible adoptive parents, she'd found
the actual process of it—the waiting and the uncer-
tainty—quite gruelling.

She'd had to list every address she'd had in her
adult life, every organization she'd ever belonged to,
and every job she'd ever had. She'd been allowed to
choose the sex and approximate age of the child she
hoped for, but that was all. Brady and Stacey must
have been through the same thing.

She'd spent weeks in fear that her application
would snag and fail on some small detail, and weeks
more, before her flight to Vietnam, panicking that she
might not be able to bond with the child who'd been
chosen for her.

She couldn't imagine how those had been good
months in Brady's life, but maybe it was a very different process if you weren't going through it alone.

"So, if you moved because of your husband's job,
that means you don't have parents or siblings here,

right?'' he asked, while she was still thinking about his last statement.

''No, no siblings anywhere,'' she told him.

His gray, thoughtful gaze was still fixed on her, and she found it unsettling. His questions were like an interview, or a test. For the sake of Colleen and Scarlett, she hid her growing anger and discomfort. What was he angling toward?

''I'm an only child,'' she explained.

''Me, too.''

''My parents divorced when I was in grade school, as I said. My mother's still in Chicago, and my Dad died when I was eighteen.''

''I'm sorry to hear that.''

''Yes, it was hard,'' she answered. It wasn't something she let herself think about.

''But at least you have your mother, not so far away.''

''Far enough!''

Mom hadn't visited since Colleen's adoption. She'd sent gifts, and she talked about coming, but she hadn't made it yet. Mom was a cautious, conservative person, slow to adjust to new situations. How would she deal with the news of Colleen's twin?

''And what about your husband's parents?'' Brady asked.

''They're in Florida. We were never all that close, and I've lost touch with them since Glenn's death.''

It all sounded too arid and distant. She knew that, and wondered what Brady would think. It wasn't her fault. She'd called Glenn's parents and sent cards for birthdays and anniversaries and holidays. But if they were out when she called and she left a message,

they never called back. They never sent cards in return, and when she'd told them about her plan to
adopt a Vietnamese baby, she could practically hear
the ice crackling down the phone. They'd considered
her action an affront to their son's memory.

This was when she'd given up. She and Colleen
would go on putting down their roots here in St. Paul.
They had a great house in a great neighborhood. She
had good friends she'd made over the past ten years,
and more friends she'd begun to make with other
mothers since adopting Colleen. They were both
happy at the day-care center, and she'd begun to consider schools for her daughter's education later on.

Brady was looking at her as if all of this—this
failure, this distance, this determined independence—was scrolling across her forehead like a Tele-
PrompTer, and as if it said as much about who she
was as did her taste in clothes. It probably did.

Their pizza arrived, along with salad and soda pop
for the adults. Brady took a knife, cut a slice of pizza
into bite-sized pieces for Scarlett, then used it to lift
a second slice onto Libby's plate, while she was occupied in helping Colleen. He had big hands, but he
used them well, with sure, economical movements.

Sliding a third slice onto his own plate, he got
some sauce on his forefinger and casually wiped it
into his mouth.

"You said you didn't want to wait before we
talked," he said. "Does that mean you already know
what you want to do?"

"It means I know what we *have* to do," she corrected him quickly. "As I see it, Brady, there's no
choice."

She took a small bite of the hot, crisp slice, but

her appetite didn't respond. Her stomach was far too churned up to feel hungry, and she was nauseous. She had a deep, instinctive dread of laying her emotional cards on the table like this, which she could never really understand. It wasn't fair to blame Glenn and the patterns that had evolved during their marriage.

"Okay, so tell me." Brady leaned forward a little, his face serious and steady.

"I don't buy your point about visits and access, like after a divorce," she began.

"No?" He looked as if he was sincerely ready to listen, and she liked that. Grabbed on to it hard, gritted her teeth, fought back the nausea, and hoped with her whole heart.

"These girls have already lost both their biological parents, whoever they were," she went on. "During the adoption ceremony in Vietnam, we undertook to keep them in touch with their cultural heritage."

"Yes, I remember that bit."

"It's going to be hard to make that more than a token thing, across a whole, huge ocean. I can't justify making their relationship with each other only a token thing, as well. The girls are way too young just to put them on a plane and send them back and forth, in any case, and there's only one way I can see to avoid doing that," she finished on a rush of words that came out more aggressively than she'd intended.

"Yeah?" He tilted his head and narrowed his eyes. His attitude had changed. He looked skeptical, now, ready to shoot first and ask questions later.

She lifted her chin, took a deep breath and just said it. "One of us is going to have to move."

* * *

Okay, Brady thought.

Hadn't he known something like that was coming? Wasn't it the only reasonable solution a sane, feeling person could come up with? It wasn't so drastic. People moved from one part of the country to another for far less meaningful reasons. And wouldn't he have said it himself, if she hadn't?

No, he wouldn't. Not yet.

He didn't like the way she'd said "one of us," and he wasn't fooled by the apologetic spread of her dainty, pretty hands as soon as she finished speaking, nor by the nervous lapping of her pink tongue against the still-glistening color on her upper lip as she waited for his response.

He took a large bite of pizza, aware that she'd barely touched her own slice.

So one of them was going to have to move? Hanging in the air, unspoken, he could almost hear her corollary, "And I'm happy and set up in St. Paul, so I don't see why it should be me."

Well, she was wrong about that.

This was why he hadn't wanted to discuss it so soon. He'd known that if she really believed in the importance of keeping the girls connected, this was the solution she'd propose. He'd seen it coming, in his own heart and in hers, but he'd wanted to wait, in the hope they'd each manage to build a little trust.

This was why he'd asked her all those questions, just now. He'd wanted to gauge the ties she had here in Minnesota, and whether there was any possible way she could justify asking *him* to uproot his life. If he moved, he would have to sell his company, deprive Scarlett of a close, loving grandmother, start over in a new state and a new town. When Libby had no family here, and could easily get a job almost anyplace she went, was it unreasonable, on his part, to expect her to make the move?

He didn't think so, and she might as well know it upfront. He wasn't going to leave himself open to emotional manipulation.

"Columbus is a great place to raise kids," he said steadily, not quite smiling. "Housing is affordable. People are friendly. Winters are mild compared to here. You're going to love it. I'll even help you with your move."

He'd made her speechless. That wasn't a bad thing. She sat there, slowly turning pink, with her pretty mouth dropped open. She looked at Colleen, looked at him, looked at Scarlett. Still didn't say a word. Closed her mouth eventually, as if she knew it was more polite, and went on saying nothing.

So maybe he should give himself more credit for his powers of speech. He knew that running his own company for the past five years had honed his ability to handle careless sub-contractors and late-paying clients.

State your position up-front and show the opposition how he or she stands to win. Build immediately on your advantage.

It seemed he'd honed his ability to handle personal relationships as well, because even now, after he'd given her plenty of time, she still didn't speak, and he still had the upper hand.

"I could see you in Upper Arlington," he went on. "Worthington, or maybe Clintonville, where I live myself. Bexley is beautiful, but that's on the other side of town from where I'm located."

"I guess it wouldn't make sense to move seven hundred miles and have the girls still end up a long drive from each other," Libby said at last. Her voice shook a little, Brady thought.

Was she trying not to cry? Yeah, he felt a little emotional, too. Both of their lives had turned upside-down today. He was still crossing his fingers that they'd each flipped in the same direction.

He waited once more for her to make some kind of a counter offer, as a potential client might do in response to his company's cost estimation on a big project.

I'll move, but not until spring.

I'll move, but it would seem fair if you covered half the expenses.

I'll move, but I'll need somewhere to stay until I can decide where I want to live, and whether I want to rent or buy. And there has to be a fall-back if it doesn't work out. I don't want to sell my house in St. Paul, and I want to get back here sometimes to see friends.

She didn't say any of that. Instead, she poured herself some more pop, and Colleen some more juice. Then she helped with Colleen's pizza.

Brady saw that her hands were shaking, and he felt an odd and powerful need to take them between his work-hardened palms and say, "Stop. It's okay. Are you upset at the thought of moving? If you feel that strongly about it, St. Paul looks like a great city, and I'll love it here."

Was that what she wanted? Were the shaking hands just a cold-blooded example of the kind of emotional manipulation he couldn't stomach? Was the silence an opportunity for her to hone her strategy? It wouldn't surprise him. Some women played their relationships like chess games. He just wished Libby would say what she felt, and say it clearly. But she didn't.

Instead, she was speaking in a bright tone to her daughter. "Let me cut that piece in half for you, honey. Yes, I know you want to do it yourself, but this bit Mommy has to help with. There you go, beautiful."

He liked the way she talked to her daughter. Sweet and steady and clear. Plenty of endearments, but not too much fussing. Suddenly he found himself making the counter offers for her. All of them. In the same clipped, confident voice he used when proposing contract terms.

"Wait till spring if you want, and count on me to cover the moving expenses," he said. "I have a pretty big place. You can stay there, with your own room and bathroom, while you decide on a permanent place. You don't need to sell your house here right away. Best for both of us if you have some fall-back in case this doesn't work out."

"You've thought it through, haven't you?" There was a note of controlled accusation in her voice.

"Didn't take long," he answered. "Most of it's obvious. Makes sense that neither of us burns our bridges. Makes sense for you to have the time you need."

"And is there a deadline on my decision?"

He shot her a closer look. Was she angry? Her voice was still just as sweet and steady. Her cheeks were still just as pink. He didn't know what to think, didn't understand what was going on in her head.

When Mom was angry or upset, she said exactly

what was on her mind. Loudly. When she tried some underhanded tactics and he confronted her with them, she confessed at once. He appreciated that.

With Stacey, in contrast, it had been like building a house on quicksand. She'd lied. She'd pretended to have emotions she didn't feel in order to get her way. She'd played on the beliefs she knew he had about duty and honor. She'd splashed around her emotions—genuine and false—like a one-year-old throwing food.

He waited for a mild, Miss Minnesota Princess version of either Mom or Stacey, but nothing happened, and this left him at a loss. Colleen shifted in her seat and looked uncomfortable. She provided a welcome change of focus. The restaurant was filling fast, and the noise level was rising, along with the smell of pizza in the oven.

"I think she's working on a diaper," Brady and Libby both said in unison.

Libby added, "I'll take her out. Eat all you want of the pizza and salad because I'm done."

"You haven't eaten very much," he pointed out, although this wasn't the issue he wanted to confront her on. "You haven't finished a single slice."

She shrugged and gave a polite smile. "I wasn't very hungry."

Holding her daughter's hand, she walked in the direction of the bathroom, still giving no indication of what she was feeling beyond her well-mannered facade.

Brady watched helplessly after her, wondering whether he'd won tonight's most important victory, Ohio State Buckeyes over Minnesota Gophers, or whether instead he'd just stared down the barrel of his own defeat.

Chapter Three

Libby shifted her life to Ohio on a Thursday in late October with Colleen, after five weeks of making lists and telephone calls and announcements, of talking to Realtors and moving companies, of packing and sorting and giving away.

Brady had told her back in September that she could "wait until spring" to make the move, as if this was some sort of a concession from him, or as if he were giving her permission, but this was her own decision, and she saw it differently. She hadn't wanted to wait. It was six months until spring, and that was a long time in a child's life.

She found all the concerned and curious questioning from friends and co-workers stressful, too, and needed a definite date on which all that would stop.

Mom had been skeptical and discouraging about the move, and had asked Libby over the phone more than once, "Is it really that important to give Colleen a sister?"

"Brady and I both think so," Libby had told her.

"But you always insisted on how self-sufficient and happy and well-adjusted you were going to be, just the two of you, even though I always thought it would be harder than you expected. Now you're doing a complete about-face."

Well, it wasn't like that, Libby considered, but she didn't say so.

Her emotional compass was pointing steadily in one direction—toward Ohio, where the girls could be sisters, where they'd have a chance to establish what could be the most enduring relationship of their lives, and where she wouldn't ever have to just send her daughter off on a plane. She couldn't predict in advance if the move would succeed or fail. She just had to jump in with both feet and do it.

To give Brady credit, he seemed to understand. "Send your stuff on ahead, and I'll arrange to be there when it arrives. I'll have your room ready for you. Let's focus on the practical things. The rest can wait."

She and Colleen took two days to make the drive from Minnesota, staying in a motel in Bloomington, Illinois, on Thursday night. Colleen awoke early the next morning, and Libby dressed her in the cute outfit she'd packed specially—a long-sleeved cotton knit dress in pink and white, high-waisted and full in the skirt, with matching leggings.

After a breakfast stop just outside Champaign, Colleen napped for three hours in the car and Libby was able to make good time. They hit Columbus midafternoon, with Miss Bright and Beautiful getting bored and fretful in her car seat after so long.

Libby could easily have fretted, also. Her legs were stiff, her head ached, her eyes felt as dry as ash. And she was nervous, with a sinking, queasy stomach and clammy hands.

Brady had given her clear directions to a neighborhood she discovered to be quiet and tree-filled. The day was smoky and cool—undeniably fall, with piles of leaves in rust and tan and orange and gold carpeting the grass beneath the bare trees. It was much milder here than it had been two days ago in St. Paul, however.

As Libby drove down Brady's street, a middle-aged man worked a leaf blower, and a helmeted child clattered along the sidewalk on a purple bicycle. She was looking for number 1654, and here it was—a house of sand-colored Ohio stone, with pale blue ornamental shutters, a steep slate roof, a sweep of gently sloping lawn out front, shaded by a couple of big trees and a fenced rear yard.

She parked in front of one half of the double garage and walked to the front door at Colleen's pace, holding her warm little hand. Almost as soon as she rang the bell, she could hear Brady's heavy footsteps, and the door opened seconds later.

''Hi.'' His eyes met hers for just a second, looking slate-blue and preoccupied, and he lifted a hand in greeting.

She was swamped with memories of the time they'd spent together in St. Paul, and didn't know what to do with them. She'd forgotten the aura of strength that surrounded him, and the way her body responded to it.

He had a cell phone pressed to his ear, and he was reeling off what sounded like building specifications. Something like that. Figures and quantities and codes. He wore jeans, a black sweatshirt and a waterproof gray jacket, as if he'd just gotten home, or was about to go out. There was no sign of his daughter.

Libby felt cold after the heated car, and she was tired, prickly and ready to find fault. Capping the upheaval of the past six weeks, she'd wanted more than a "hi" and a glance, and she hadn't wanted the powerful pull Brady seemed to exert on her body without even trying.

Now he was nodding, listening to the voice at the other end of the line, trying to get a word in. "Yes…yes, Nate. I got that. You tell me what you have, okay?"

Libby picked up Colleen.

Still listening and saying, "Yes," every few seconds, Brady stepped back, reached around to flatten a hand between her shoulder blades, and pulled her inside.

He had big hands, and his touch was warm and heavy on her back. Her shoulder nudged the curve where his arm met his body and she remembered too many moments back in Minnesota when she'd felt this pull and this awareness.

He had that same earthy, resinous smell that she'd first noticed, like fresh-cut wood, and the same faint sheen of reddish beard just beginning to grow out against his rugged skin. As she passed him, moving ahead into the hall, she could easily have reached out and brushed her hand across that strong, square jaw.

She wasn't usually so conscious of how her body

shaped itself near a man's, and of how the air moved between them. And she couldn't remember when she'd last wanted to inhale a man's scent like inhaling the fresh air of spring. But then, there weren't many men in her life that she ever got this close to. Under the circumstances, it was hardly surprising if she felt jittery and hypersensitive.

He kicked the door shut behind him and said, as an aside from his phone conversation, "Stairs. Go on up, Libby. All the way to the end." To her new, temporary room.

He followed her, still absorbed in his call, and he didn't end it until they reached the room's closed door, when his firm footsteps stopped just behind her.

"Sorry about that," he said at last, flipping the phone shut and sliding it into his back pocket. "I took today off to get the house ready for you, but they can't leave me alone. We have a big project that's running behind schedule. It's not important."

"Sounds like it is." She stepped sideways, with Colleen still in her arms, and angled herself so that Brady wasn't looming over her shoulder.

He gave a rueful smile that crinkled the skin around his eyes and showed straight white teeth. "Well, it's not *important* important."

Libby smiled, too. "A subtle yet critical difference, I guess. Where's Scarlett?" she added on a rush.

She felt a fluttery anticipation about seeing Colleen's twin that she tried to dampen down. It didn't feel safe to start to care so soon and so much.

"Mom has her on Fridays," Brady answered.

He flattened a hand against his back pocket, as if to check that his cell phone was there. It was an unnecessary gesture, since he'd put it there just seconds ago. He was on edge, just as she was. His strong shoulders were held tight, and he curled his hands into fists then let them go again.

"She works Monday through Thursday," he went on. "So on those days Scarlett's in day care. You're earlier than I was expecting. I was just about to go pick her up from Mom's. Here…" He opened the door.

It was a big room, built over the whole area of the double garage, and it was lit by large windows on three sides. The white drapes looked new. Libby recognized her own queen-sized oak sleigh bed, with matching tallboy and dresser, her own delicately flower-sprigged sheet set, comforter and pillows, and the oak glider-rocker she'd bought last year, for sitting in to feed a bottle to Colleen.

Brady had angled the rocker so that it would get bathed in southern winter sun, and the matching oak crib was right next to it, made up with Colleen's white broderie anglaise bed linen.

Finally, on top of the tallboy, sitting on a plastic place-mat, there was a pewter beer tankard stuffed— yes, you'd have to call it stuffed—with a big bunch of supermarket flowers, still swathed in their silver wrapping.

"Anything you want moved," Brady offered, "just say so."

"No, it looks good." Apart from the supermarket sticker on the flowers.

The flowers said a lot. He must have remembered she liked to have them around the house. He'd taken the trouble to buy some. But he didn't have a clue how to arrange them, and he didn't even own a proper vase. The mix of thoughtfulness and clumsiness somehow softened her heart to a dangerous level.

They were both trying so hard.

So hard.

That had to be a good thing, didn't it?

"It's a great room," she told him, meaning it.

"There's a bathroom right next door that's just for you."

"You didn't have to make the bed."

He shrugged. "You moved your life seven-hundred-odd miles. I made a bed. Are we even yet?"

She laughed, and it eased a little of the awkwardness in the air. Colleen wriggled out of her arms, toddled forward and launched herself at the rocking chair. Her fat, diaper-wrapped bottom stuck out and she buried her face in the cushion seat. She was attached to this chair, and Libby was grateful for the presence of the familiar object. All of this had to be confusing for a young child. It was confusing enough for an adult!

"Let me help unload your car, then I'll go get Scarlett," Brady said, watching Lisa-Belle watch Colleen.

He felt that they needed both girls here, blatantly identical, to remind them of why they were putting themselves through this. It was awkward. No doubt about that. He'd had Nate badgering him in one ear when she arrived. He hadn't known what to say to her.

Welcome to my life?

And the flowers were probably dumb.

"Are you hungry?" he said, his voice gruff. "I

could fix you coffee and a snack and you and Colleen can eat while I unpack.''

''I'm fine. I'm not leaving all the unpacking to you.''

No, Libby, honey, you missed your cue.

He'd been trying to give them both an out, a way not to have to eyeball each other as they went back and forth with boxes and bags for the next ten minutes. She hadn't taken it. He tried again. ''Or take a shower if you want.''

''Tonight. Not now.'' She was too wrapped inside her own tension to perceive her wide-open escape route. ''We should unpack.''

Colleen followed her mommy back and forth, threatening a couple of times to trip Brady up as he came in the opposite direction. He had to watch out for her underfoot, and he had to be careful, but he knew Scarlett would have done the exact same thing in an unfamiliar situation. Both girls were a little clingy.

Libby distracted him. She was petite, but she didn't play helpless. She did her share. As he approached the car for his second load, he saw her leaning into the back seat to pick up a box, her bottom taut and round beneath a floral skirt that somehow managed to be both soft and flowing and sexily clingy at the same time. His body stirred and his blood felt as heavy as lead.

Ah, hell! This again!

This attraction that he didn't want. The mechanics of male anatomy were a damned nuisance, sometimes. What would she think if she knew he was looking at her this way? How was he going to handle it, having her sleeping under his roof, maybe for weeks?

It had become clear during the day and a half he'd spent in Minnesota that she wasn't involved with anyone there, and it must be pretty obvious to her that he hadn't dated since Stacey's death. Physically, his needs tormented him at times, but emotionally he felt only reluctance about any kind of involvement, and so in that area he was very much alone.

On paper, therefore, they were both free to leap into bed with each other tonight, as soon as the girls were asleep.

Who would know?

Whose business would it be, anyhow?

But he didn't believe you could put sex in its own little compartment that didn't impinge on the rest of your life, even if that was a convenient theory for some men, and he was sure that Libby wouldn't believe it, either.

Sex mattered. Even sharing a kitchen could matter.

They had the girls to consider. They had to create a workable, co-operative relationship that would survive the next twenty years, and if they stuffed it up with sex and domestic illusions and a short-lived affair right at the beginning, it would be their daughters who would suffer the most.

He should have given Libby the phone number of one of the motels along Olentangy River Road and left her to fend for herself, honor and duty be damned. It might have been a necessary protection for both of them.

The car was full. Several suitcases, those boxes, and what looked like a big styrofoam cooler that Libby carried through the house and into the kitchen at the back. Two of the boxes she wanted in the kitchen as well.

"What's in these?" he asked.

"Pantry goods. I thought I might as well bring them rather than throwing them out."

"And in the cooler?"

"Frozen casseroles. Chicken and mushroom. Burgundy beef. Irish stew."

Brady's mouth began to water. So she cooked. She actually cooked. Having tasted her baking the day they'd first met, he was in no doubt whatsoever that she would cook well, and he hadn't eaten a woman's home-cooked meal in so long he could hardly remember what it was like.

Mom used to slap together a few easy recipes several nights in the week when he was a kid, but she'd stopped altogether when Dad had died ten years ago. She ate strange little evening meals now, like cottage cheese and sliced banana on toast, or canned soup in a mug. She was a big fan of the drive-through window at the local fast-food chain, too. Now that Scarlett had outgrown jars of baby food, so was Brady.

Burgundy beef, on the other hand... Shoot, but that sounded good!

"We could have one of them tonight, if you don't have anything planned," Libby offered.

Uh, no, he didn't have anything planned.

He told her so, while realizing that he should have planned a whole lot of things. So that they didn't have to confront the weird reality of their new situation. If either of them made too many mistakes at the beginning, their commitment to putting their daughters' relationship first might show up as impossibly naive and unworkable.

They could end up in court, hating each other. That guilty wish—Libby had admitted to it, as well—that his mom had never seen Colleen's photo in that magazine might turn into a bitter, lifelong and reasoned regret.

"I'll put two of these in the freezer and leave the third to thaw," Libby said.

"Burgundy beef sounds good," he suggested, a little embarrassed at the eagerness that immediately crept into his voice.

She smiled. "Burgundy beef it is, then."

The sun struggled through a thin patch in the low, smoky cloud at that moment and the kitchen lit up, striking her blond hair, giving that melted-candy look to her pretty mouth. His blood slowed and his groin stirred again.

He was hungry. Not burgundy-beef hungry, but candy hungry, hungry for a woman's sweet, melting mouth, hungry for her soft skin, for the touch of her fingers and the press of her breasts. Hungry for *this* woman. Just because she was here?

"I'll go pick up Scarlett," he said abruptly. Libby was staring at him, lips parted, eyes startled and swimming with heat. "Please make yourselves at home." He grabbed his keys from a pocket, headed out the side door and let out a sigh of relief as soon as he reached the steps.

Chapter Four

"Make yourselves at home?" Libby muttered, after Brady had gone.

For how long would they need to do that? A week? A month? There was a pile of newspapers on the table in the breakfast nook, and she realized that he must have been collecting and saving the real estate section from the *Columbus Dispatch* for her, for the past three or four weeks. Flipping through the top copy, she saw that he'd circled a few places with a yellow highlighter pen.

Thoughtful.

Or was he just trying to get rid of her fast? She supported that plan. Standing in the kitchen together just now, the current between them had almost glowed. Her spine still tingled. Her breasts still ached. When she wrapped her arms around herself, it was his heat that she felt.

Colleen tugged at her skirt. "Fir-sty," she said.

"You're thirsty, honey?"

"'N hundwy, too."

"Let's see what we've got."

There was milk in the fridge. Not a lot else.

She remembered some packets of peanut butter crackers in one of the pantry boxes and dug them out, looked around and discovered Colleen's own high chair sitting beside Scarlett's in a corner of the big kitchen. Libby slid the high chair out from the wall and lifted Colleen into it, and Colleen seemed quite happy to accept that it was here.

Hello, chair.

Libby peered through to the living room. There was none of her stuff in here. In the end, she'd rented her house out partly furnished to some friends who were renovating their own place, and she'd only brought enough to furnish a modest apartment here in Columbus. It was part of the not-burning-her-boats strategy she and Brady had both agreed on. She'd have to fly home in a couple of months to make a more long-term arrangement, but she didn't want to think about that yet.

Brady's living room was very masculine, furnished with brown leather sofas—a two-seater, a three-seater and an armchair—a large, low, heavy-looking coffee table made of dark wood, a square of Persian carpet on the hardwood floor, an open fireplace and a series of framed, limited edition photos of spectacular moments in sport.

The photos were just about the last thing in the world she would have chosen to put her own walls, but they were high-quality pictures, expertly hung, and the effect was far more attractive and dramatic than she would have expected. She actually liked it.

Colleen banged her cup on her chair tray and started singing, and Libby ducked back into the kitchen to make sure she wasn't trying to climb out. That day would come soon. Now there were going to be two such bold little girls, pushing the boundaries of parental fear in this way. Examining the industrial-strength safety harness Brady had attached to Scarlett's high chair, Libby was in no doubt that Colleen's twin must be attempting Houdini-like feats.

Brady hadn't said how long he expected to be. Libby phoned Chicago to let her mom know that she and Colleen had safely arrived. To get off to a good start, she also called a few numbers on the list of gynecology specialists that her St. Paul ob/gyn practice had given her and managed to get an appointment with the third one on the list for a Monday afternoon, two and a half weeks away.

If she was going to build a successful life here, she wasn't going to let the grass grow under her feet when it came to practical details. She'd been meaning to make this particular appointment for a while, but somehow hadn't gotten to it before she left. To be honest, she'd been putting it off.

Colleen finished her snack and clamored to be let down. After reminding her of the existence of "please," Libby complied. Once again, she felt restless and jittery, and Colleen was getting antsy now, too, wanting to explore.

Together, they started unpacking the pantry boxes, finding the shelf where Brady kept cereal, and the one where he kept canned goods. If this was "making themselves at home'' to a greater degree than he'd intended, he'd have to tell her so.

She heard the hum and rumble of his garage door about fifteen minutes later, and he soon appeared at the side door, with Scarlett in his arms. She was dressed in denim overalls with a red sweater beneath, and Libby wanted to hold her and hug her and tell her, ''Guess what? You have a mommy now!''

She didn't do it. She was too scared, and anyhow for Scarlett it would have been way too soon.

When was the awkwardness going to subside?

The girls just stared at each other. Sisters? They were strangers! Brady took in the peanut butter cracker crumbs on the high chair, the sippy cup on the sink, the open pantry door and the plastic storage container of burgundy beef on the counter-top. It had started leaking melted freezer frost onto the duck-egg-green formica.

''I was just—'' Libby began.

''It's fine. Scarlett had a big snack at Mom's.'' He looked at his watch and frowned.

Could I cut this air with a knife, or what? Brady thought.

His watch confirmed that at least three hours remained until they could put the girls to bed, and probably five or six until Libby would want to hit the hay herself. He'd spent several minutes at Mom's convincing her, not for the first time, that she couldn't rush over here right now to scoop Colleen into her arms. As far as she was concerned, she had a second grandchild now, and she was just as excited as she'd been when he and Stacey had brought Scarlett home. Maybe even more so.

"And why can't I come over?" she'd wanted to know, as if he hadn't been through all this with her before.

"It wouldn't be fair to Lisa-Belle," he'd said. "Or to Colleen."

Problem was, he wasn't good at articulating this kind of stuff. It really wouldn't be fair. There were reasons, but he couldn't pin them down in words. Fatigue. Overload. Take it slow. Give them time. Don't scare them, when this is already scary enough.

And now they were just standing here, face-to-face—Libby's eyes were so big and blue and pretty—and neither of them knew what to say or do next. He'd been absent a little longer than he wanted. The traffic cops had just closed off Lane Avenue for the annual Ohio State University Fall Homecoming Parade, and the traffic was heavier than usual, coming back from Grandview, up Route 315.

"Listen," he said on an impulse he didn't stop to rethink. "Would you like some fresh air and a little exercise? The Homecoming Parade is on soon. It's hokey, but it's fun. They throw candy from the floats, and wind up with the marching band coming past, and it really is the Best Damned Band In the Land, so it can be fun."

"Yes, let's do that. It sounds nice." She grinned, looking relieved, which confirmed his sense that she'd felt as uncomfortable as he was about what to do next, reluctant to leave any space for the electricity to come crackling back into the air. "Although I should tell you," she added, "we have a pretty good college marching band at home, too."

"Don't even start," he threatened, grinning wider

than she was. "You're talking to a die-hard Buckeye, remember?"

"So when should we go?"

"Five minutes? Is that too soon for you? We'll have to park north of campus, get the girls in their coats and hats, and strapped in their strollers. It's chilling down out there. We'll go in my car, so you'll need to shift Colleen's car seat, too. Maybe we don't have time for this, after all..."

"Shifting her seat'll only take a minute. I left our coats in the bedroom upstairs, and I'm going to change into some pants, if we'll be standing around in the dark."

The imminent prospect of getting out of the house energized and de-stressed them both, and the girls picked up on the atmosphere at once. Scarlett refused to get into her coat and wanted to turn it into a game of chase. She toddled at her usual breakneck speed around the circuit of living room to hall to kitchen and through to the living room again, shrieking with laughter.

Brady let her get away with it and pretended he couldn't catch up to her. Finally, he cornered her by the side table in the front hall when, helpless with hiccupping laughs, she tripped over her own feet.

"Got you! Now I'm going to wrap you up in a parcel so tight, you'll never get loose," he threatened, then saw Colleen watching the two of them with her big, dark eyes, through the wooden spindles of the stair rail. She'd retreated to a position several steps up.

"Want to play, too?" he offered.

His heart gave that little lurch he'd only just begun to get used to. He had two daughters, now, only this one didn't understand that, yet, and she was a little nervous away from her own territory. He was only beginning to understand it himself, and didn't push Colleen to get over her shyness. It would take time.

Libby came down a couple of minutes later, while Colleen was still sitting on the stairs. Libby wore jeans that hugged her legs and hips the way frosting hugged the top of a cake, and a stretchy top with long sleeves and a wide, round neck, covered in a sprinkle of flowers.

There was a row of pearly little buttons running down the front of the top. They didn't run all the way. They stopped right between her delicious, rounded breasts—and so did his gaze. One open button, and he'd be able to see a shadow, two and he'd be able to bury his face there and taste her skin. Sweet jiminy!

Enough, Brady, he coached himself. Enough!

She had her puffy, pale gray coat hanging over her arm and Colleen's much smaller pink-and-purple one dangling in one hand. As long as Libby put her coat on soon—

What? He might survive until she took it off again?

He had to do a heck of a lot better than that! For the next…what, week? month?…they would be living together.

His cell phone rang, pealing out some candy-flavored tune which his office manager, Gretchen Taylor, had programmed in for him and which he couldn't be bothered to change. He saw the way Libby schooled her face into a neat picture of patience and sat down on the stairs beside Colleen, and then he heard Gretchen's voice at the other end of the line.

She sounded stressed. "Nate hasn't shown up yet."

"No? He should get there any minute, from what he said earlier."

"It's after five. I wanted to get home. I hate leaving Alison on her own."

"I know, Gretchen."

In the background, Scarlett drummed her heels exuberantly on the floor.

"...So what do you want me to do?"

He tried not to sigh audibly into the phone. Nate Simmons had dated Gretchen for a while. She was a few years older than Nate was, with a twelve-year-old daughter. They'd broken up after a couple of months. Brady didn't know why, and he wasn't going to ask.

Now Gretchen had this aggrieved sub-text going on every time she spoke to him about Nate, as if she expected Brady himself to do something about it. He gave her what she wanted, at least on a micromanagement level.

"Go home," he told her. "The rest can wait until Monday."

Messy office romances killed him, but how could you prevent that stuff? He didn't believe you could forbid it, the way some corporations tried to do. It'd be worse if people started sneaking around. He just wished they would look a little harder before they leapt in.

Remember that, Brady. Keep your own rule, and stop looking so hard at the wrong parts of Libby McGraw.

"Okay, Brady." Gretchen wasn't as diplomatic as he'd tried to be in controlling her sigh. It practically whooshed out of the earpiece of his phone and whistled right through his head. "I'll see you Monday," she said. "Have a good weekend."

"Yeah. Thanks."

Yeah. Yeah. He'd try. He might burst into flames first.

He hadn't told anyone at the office or anyone on his sites about Scarlett's twin. Not yet. He planned to wait a couple of weeks, see how the chips fell. And it would probably be best if he waited until Libby and Colleen were out of his house, too. Then he'd gather his senior people together and make an announcement, as low-key as possible, then leave them to spread the news however they wanted. He hoped this was the best way to handle it. There were no precedents to fall back on.

As soon as he'd gotten back from Minnesota, he'd told a couple of college friends, Matt and Russ—the ones he watched football with—and they had initially come out with a less-than-helpful repertoire of stunned expletives. In the weeks since, however, they'd done some more of the nice male friendship stuff they'd been doing since Stacey's accident, like coming round in the evenings with pizzas, videos and beer, and helping him lop some big branches off an unsafe tree in the yard on a weekend. That was great, but it didn't provide him with any answers.

He'd asked them to stay away for the next couple of weeks until "things got settled." Now he wondered if a continuation of the pizzas and videos and beer might have diluted the intensity of the air between himself and Libby a little.

"Sorry," he told her, after he'd ended the phone call. She was still sitting on the stairs, hugging Colleen.

"I guess it's what happens when you run your own business," she said. "Thanks for taking today off. I appreciate it."

"Watch me, I'm switching off the cell phone. Let's go before Nate tries to get me on the land line."

They got the girls strapped in their seats and drove the short distance down to the North Campus area. Brady found parking without too much trouble. On football Saturdays, it would have been a different story.

The floats had already started coming past when they reached a vantage point on the corner of Lane and Neil avenues. It was still light, with the sun coloring up the west, painting this year's top interior design shades onto the wall of breaking clouds.

Brady hadn't managed to get to this event for the past few years, but the parade was pretty much the same as it had always been. Homecoming king and queen and courtiers in vintage cars, kids still in their teens tossing handfuls of candy from antique fire trucks and amateur floats. The marching band was the highlight and the reason Brady came when he could.

Libby apparently heard the drums in the distance and pricked up her ears. She had the collar of her coat turned up and a soft pink-and-gray hat, shaped like a bell, jammed down on her head. Her cheeks were pink from the cold and her eyes were bright and interested.

The girls both loved the candy. Colleen hardly

seemed to know what it was—Libby was obviously
careful about nutrition—but she wanted it anyway,
every time it flew in her direction. In contrast, with
a grandmother who regarded spoiling as a God-given
right, Scarlett probably knew far too much about the
stuff.

Released from their strollers, the two of them
rushed around squealing and picking up Tootsie
Rolls and lollipops, their arms a little stiff, one in a
pink-and-purple coat and one in a fleece-lined denim
jacket. Their hands were soon crammed and spilling
over.

Libby took off her hat, making golden strands of
hair fluff up in a halo around her head. "Put it in
here, guys," she told them, and they ran back and
forth, cadging the stuff from adult candy collectors.
They were just too cute to resist, and they didn't even
know it.

Libby's hat was full in minutes. She held it out to
Brady, laughing. "What do I do now?"

Brady was bare-headed, but he had pockets—
slanty jacket pockets which turned out to be almost
impossible to fill. They tried anyway, spilling it from
the hat crown as they tipped it in.

"This isn't working," Libby said.

She took a handful instead, held the pocket open
and thrust her cache inside. The jacket tugged and
tightened at his shoulder with the push of her hand,
and Brady realized that their heads were almost
touching.

The corner of her coat collar brushed across his
cheek, and when she rummaged in the hat for another
handful of candy, he felt her shoulder nudge his arm
and her hip bump his thigh. He was badly tempted

to get even closer, to find out how soft that hair felt against the brush of his mouth. Just a little moment like this, and his whole body was throbbing.

Stop this!

"Okay, now I have room for some more," she said, and stepped away.

The band got nearer and louder, and there were some sporadic cheers and calls from farther along. Brady could hear the classic, familiar drum riff like a call to arms, making Buckeye blood beat faster in Buckeye veins across the whole state. What were the team's chances of making it to the Rose Bowl championship this year?

"They're adorable," an older woman said beside him, her voice gushy and high. She wasn't talking about the football team, or even the band. "And they're *identical!* How come you dress 'em so different?"

"Uh, so we can tell them apart." He was improvising, and it showed. His and Libby's diametrically opposing views on how to dress their girls was an issue they hadn't begun to tackle. Would they eventually have to? Or could they agree to differ?

As for the woman's clear assumption that they were married...

"Really?" she said. "And you're their parents! My Lord!" She took another look at the girls, but seemed to accept his statement. "They really are identical," she repeated. "What a cute, cute family."

"Thanks," he muttered.

"Adopted, of course." She was looking at Lisa-Belle, now, taking in her Scandinavian fairness.

"Yes." He felt uncomfortable, and was glad when the woman turned away.

Libby was trying to corral both girls and keep them within reach. Hampered by a hat once more brimming to overflow point with candy, she was having a hard time.

"Colleen, honey, stay with Mommy. Scarlett, stay with—" she took a jerky breath "—with me."

To Scarlett, she wasn't Mommy. Not yet. Brady didn't blame her for that. But it was another future hurdle to get across.

The band had almost reached them, pushing a wave of energy ahead of the long column of black-and-red-uniformed marchers and musicians. The girls were getting wild.

"Do we follow along?" Libby yelled.

"If you'd like to."

"Oh, I would! And the girls sure are raring to go."

Scarlett didn't want to go in the stroller, a sentiment which made perfect sense to Brady. She wanted to *see*. He folded the stroller quickly and swung her up to sit on his shoulders, with her arms wrapping around his forehead. Libby dumped the candy-filled hat in the seat of the other stroller, lifted Colleen onto her hip and managed to push the stroller ahead of her, one-handed.

The band broke into a double-time strut and they raced along beside it, slowing when it slowed, walking in time to its beat, surfing the excitement. Only when the column turned south into High Street did Libby stop and look at him, with a question in her eyes. She was a little breathless, and her arm had to be aching from carrying Colleen that way for so long.

"Do we keep on?" she asked.

"Let's leave it to the undergrads, now."

The girls still had energy to burn. Scarlett recognized the opportunity for one of her favorite activities when they came past a low brick wall. "Ba'ance! Ba'ance!" she said.

He put her down and held her hand and she balanced all the way along. As soon as Colleen saw, she wanted to do the same. Libby had trouble managing her and the stroller, so Brady folded it up, hat and candy still wedged and bulging, packaged by the canvas seat. He carried both folded strollers under his arm, and the girls "balanced" for a good five minutes.

"The parade was great!" Libby said.

"It's the right speed for them, isn't it?"

"For me, too."

"Yes, it's not a big enough event to draw a huge crowd, so you don't have to stand around and wait, or try to maneuver for a line of sight when the sidewalks are ten people deep, like most parades."

"It's given me an appetite."

"Someone mentioned a beef casserole, earlier."

"Someone else has to get us home, and then I think there's plenty. It shouldn't take too long to heat in the microwave. Thanks, Brady. This helped, didn't it? It was—it was awkward when I first arrived."

Yeah, awkward. That was one word for it.

He could think of a few others that fitted better.

Her blue eyes were serious, fixed on his face, asking for something from him that he didn't quite understand. Her cheeks were pink and satin-smooth from the evening cold. Her lips were full, and her mouth closed and straightened as soon as she finished speaking.

"It, uh, yeah..." he said. Didn't know quite how to answer her. "Don't know if you saw, but I left the real estate listings on the table. I circled a few things, but of course you'll want to look through them yourself. If you want to look at some places on the weekend, I can watch Colleen.''

The suggestion seemed logical, to give the girls some time together, get this sister thing going. But Libby shook her head.

"No, I'll take her with me," she answered quickly. "It's fine. It'll slow me down a little, I guess, but I'd like to see how she reacts to the places, anyhow.''

She didn't quite trust him, Brady realized, and she was making excuses.

The fact was pretty apparent—due to her own self-conscious awareness that she was making excuses, mainly. Maybe she thought he wouldn't be vigilant enough about falls and sharp objects, or that he'd give Colleen too much junk to eat. He decided to let it go for the moment. After all, how would he have felt about leaving Scarlett with Libby?

He thought about it.

No, actually, he'd have been okay with that. He'd have forced himself to be okay with it on principle. Sure, he had fears and suspicious instincts, but they'd made a commitment to bring the girls together, and he was going to act on it. He wasn't going to play emotional games, because he hated them.

At this stage, it was a little thing, but when he told himself he was letting it go, he knew in his heart that this wasn't quite true. He was storing it up, ready to be wary or angry if it happened again, ready to feel some mistrust of his own, for his own reasons.

Chapter Five

Both girls were asleep.

Scarlett had napped less and had a busier day than Colleen, so she was ready to go first, while it was after eight by the time Libby came back down the stairs. She and Brady hadn't eaten, yet. Since it was already late when they'd arrived home, they'd fed the girls first and gone through their separate, different bedtime routines. Scarlett had a bed-time story, while Colleen got a bath and songs. Singing seemed to settle her at night better than words and pictures.

Maybe singing settled Brady, too. He had the radio tuned softly to a country music station in the kitchen, and he was setting the table in the breakfast nook with place mats and cloth napkins, a bowl of bread rolls and a bottle of wine. It was a little more lavish than Libby had expected, and he caught her look of surprise.

"Figured I should do justice to the casserole," he said. "It's your first meal here."

"You haven't tasted it, yet."

"Yes, I have. I pinched a mouthful of Scarlett's. It was good. She wolfed it down. The wine's an optional extra."

"It's a French dish. The French would have it with wine."

"Gotta do what the French do," he mocked her lightly.

"You think I'm making excuses? I'll gladly drink a glass of wine without one!"

"Sometimes excuses are okay." The words were slow, a little reluctant. "You don't want to start hearing them too often, or you start to wonder what's going on…"

Libby pretended absorption in opening the wine, and didn't answer. If he meant the way she'd turned down his baby-sitting offer, she wasn't ready to admit to that yet. You couldn't force trust, and she wasn't going to apologize for not fully feeling it after so short a time. She was only sorry she hadn't managed to hide her attitude more successfully.

Let it slide, please, Brady, she begged him silently. Recognize the value of the occasional little white lie, until we know each other better.

He turned off the radio and brought the casserole to the table, steaming in a big dish, and they sat opposite each other. The breakfast nook was small, old-fashioned and pretty, set adjacent to the windows and containing a built-in wooden table and hinged bench seats with storage space underneath.

Brady looked as if another inch or two of teenage growth would have made him unable to fit in it, and

Libby had to pivot her knees a little to the side to keep her legs clear of his. She could tell by the twist in his upper body that he was doing the same thing in the opposite direction. They were, each of them, unnaturally careful about it.

He poured wine into the glasses, and pushed the bowl of crusty rolls toward her, then he sat back a little so that she had a clear run at the bread without the risk that they'd accidentally touch. This was already too much like a date—a first date between two teenagers who'd been aware of each other for a while, but didn't have the slightest clue what to say and how to act, now that they were alone.

When he grabbed his wineglass, his hand looked so tight she almost expected the fragile glass stem to snap.

"So, the weekend," he said.

"Do you have commitments?"

"I kept it clear. In case you needed help with anything."

It was the same rough-hewn kind of thoughtfulness he'd shown with the flowers in her room. She valued that. And yet she'd already turned down his offer of baby-sitting because she didn't know whether to trust him with her daughter. She felt bad about that—bad about being so unsubtle, but not bad enough to change her mind.

And is Scarlett my daughter, too? What will happen if I let myself love her as much as I love Colleen, but have no parental rights where she's concerned? If I lost her...

Too frightening to think about.

"The rest of my furniture and boxes that were shipped—" she started to say.

"In the garage and the tool room."

"So if I find somewhere to live right away…"

"I can get a van and a couple of my guys, no problem. You know there's no hurry for you to settle on anything, though."

"I appreciate that, Brady."

But…

There was a but, though neither of them mentioned it.

But if things continued to be this awkward…

Why were things this awkward?

Easy.

Because, on top of everything else, they were attracted to each other. It had begun within their first few minutes of meeting, and it hadn't gone away, it had only gotten stronger. Unlike those imaginary teenage first-daters she'd conjured up, however, they didn't want it. It added a complication to the question of the relationship between their daughters that would only get in the way. It was dangerous. There were a thousand ways in which it could end badly.

Knowing this gave Libby absolutely no power to do anything about it. She was still almost painfully conscious of the way the light hit Brady's hair and face, conscious of the contours of his shoulders, and of the movements of his hands, conscious of the way he smelled and the way he smiled.

Her senses seemed heightened in their perceptions. His voice was like rough music to her ears, and the scent of him was like the cedar balls she put in her clothing drawers.

She wanted to reach out and touch him. Just his hands at first. No hurry, no impatience. She wanted to explore the raised shapes of bone and vessel across the backs, and feel the work-hardened roughness of his palm against hers.

How would he return her touch? Would his hand engulf hers, strong and warm, or would his caress be light and teasing and slow?

"This is very, very good," Brady said.

He was talking about her Burgundy beef, not her body or the chemistry it generated with his. She liked the way he ate, hungry and appreciative but with manners that were obviously ingrained, not put on just for tonight. He'd been well raised.

"You have to use the right cut of meat," she answered. She hardly knew what she was saying. "And the right herbs, and cook it real slow."

"You're not going to narrate me the recipe, are you?"

"Well, no, I—"

She caught his expression, realized he was teasing her, and laughed. So did he. He had just the right laugh, rich and sexy and low. It was the laugh of a naughty little boy grown into a good man—the kind of man you knew still had a streak of that naughty boy hiding somewhere deep inside him, ready to dare you and tempt you into things you shouldn't want to do, but did.

She was going to bed early tonight, she decided, and she wasn't drinking any more wine. There was a book in her bag. She'd tell him she was tired, which was true, and she'd read in bed for a while, until fatigue overcame her. Brady Buchanan was the last person she wanted to be thinking of as she drifted off to sleep.

The weekend proved easier than Libby had feared. Brady got a list of suggested items from her and went out grocery shopping with Scarlett in the morning. Libby tried to give him some money for the groceries, but he wouldn't take it.

While he and Scarlett were out, Libby went through the real estate rental listings and the want ads. There was always a demand for qualified child-care staff, but she was shopping for a good environment for Colleen, also, and she didn't want to end up in some baby-minding factory on the far side of town.

Knowing little about the layout of the city, it took her a long time to go through all the listings and identify the most likely ones to try. She finished up with a list of several apartments and small houses that looked promising, and made some phone calls to arrange to see them. Tonight, she would ask if she could use Brady's computer to print out copies of her résumé, so she could call several places about employment on Monday.

While she studied maps and newspapers, Colleen was happy to play. Scarlett had some cool toys.

Brady brought pre-made, cling-wrap-covered pizzas back from the supermarket, and they all ate lunch together. Libby and Colleen had to hurry off as soon as they'd finished eating, to see the first apartment on their list. Scarlett and Brady were going to the football game.

The rental properties were the weekend's big disappointment. "The place I liked best was snapped up by the couple who got there just before me." Libby told Brady when she returned at five. "There was a nice duplex. What's it called here? A half-double? But I'm not sure about it, because it was pretty close to campus.''

''Can get a lot of late-night partying down there,'' Brady agreed.

''The best garden apartment complex only had a three-bedroom available right now, and that's too big and too expensive. The agent says she'll contact me if a two-bedroom comes up. The other places I looked at all had problems.''

''So I don't get to turf you out of here, yet?''

''No, but I'll keep you posted. We don't want to stretch this out too long.''

He didn't answer her directly, and she was glad. If they didn't admit to the way they were feeling, it would go away. She hoped. ''Have some coffee,'' Brady said instead. He was drinking a mug of it himself, and prepared to pour her one from the half-filled pot still sitting on the coffee machine's warming plate.

''Is it decaf?''

''It's mountain-grown premium Kenya blend, but no, it's not decaf.''

''Then I'll pass.''

''I can easily—''

''No, please. I'm fine.''

She went across to the sink instead and filled a glass with cold water from the faucet. Brady stood and watched, as if he was humoring her in some strange behavior. From her peripheral vision, she saw him bring his mug to his lips and take a big gulp, and she found his thoughtful silence far more powerful than words.

''Mom cracked today,'' he said, when she'd drained the glass. ''She called this afternoon, just after Scarlett and I got home. She wants to meet Colleen *this minute* because she's going crazy, yada yada. She's taking us out to dinner tonight at a Mexican restaurant near her place, and she's not taking no for an answer. If that's okay with you, of course,'' he finished.

Libby laughed. "And if it isn't?"

"Then she'll probably buy an infra-red camera and satellite tracking devices and start stalking you."

"Fun for all of us!"

"No, seriously, she's not scary. She's just a mom. I shouldn't be teasing you about her."

"I think I can handle a mom."

"So you'll come?"

"I want to meet Colleen's second grandmother, as much as she wants to meet Colleen."

Even though every new relationship we make increases the potential for pain.

The restaurant was noisy, and the food was good. Delia Buchanan had gasped and pressed her hand over her heart when she first saw Colleen. She remained a little shell-shocked throughout the meal, even though she admitted this didn't make sense.

"I mean, I knew they were identical," she said as they ate. She was a strong-boned woman, with her hair tinted a soft light brown and an alert expression behind her squarish, wire-framed glasses. "I'm the one who first saw the photo, and it never entered my head that it might not be Scarlett, even though I knew Brady loathed the idea of baby beauty pageants." Libby flushed, and Mrs. Buchanan seemed to realize she hadn't been very tactful. She went on quickly, "Not that this was a—"

"It's fine," Libby said. She'd endured criticisms of her decisions and choices that were far worse.

"And of course with her—with both of them—being so adorable, I can see exactly why you entered her. I mean, it was a talent contest as much as anything."

"It's fine," she repeated, and Brady looked at her across the corner of the table that separated them and frowned.

"I hope you can make this work," Mrs. Buchanan finished. "It's going to take some courage, and some luck."

"Mom speaks her mind," Brady said later, when they got home.

"It didn't spook me too much."

"You sure about that?" His intent gaze made her nervous.

"It was fine."

"Yeah, I guess it would be," he muttered, and Libby could see that her assurance had angered him, although she didn't know why.

On Sunday afternoon, they took the girls to Whetstone playground and the Park of Roses. There weren't any of those in bloom at this time of the year, of course. The bushes were all pruned back. There weren't many people, either, since the day was dull and cold, and this saved them from difficult questions and mistaken assumptions about their marital status by friendly strangers.

At home, Libby cooked spaghetti for dinner while Brady did something with tools in the room at the back of the garage that was crowded with her furniture, and they both pretended that they weren't avoiding each other.

It was much easier during the week.

Brady went through his usual routine with Scarlett at breakfast on Monday, and he and his daughter and Libby and hers, meshed just fine. At seven, he left the house to drop Scarlett at day care on his way to a construction site, after a quick, ''We're heading out,'' to Libby, who was down in the basement putting laundry into the machine.

''Okay, we'll see you tonight,'' she called back.

''Would you like me to ask about spaces in their casual day-care program?'' he offered, stepping onto the landing at the top of the stairs. ''You might want to put Colleen in for a few hours this week, so you can get through your errands faster.''

''I might need to,'' she agreed, although she was a little reluctant.

This didn't make sense. She was gaining a daughter, not losing one, but she felt extra protective of her relationship with Colleen at the moment, and terrified about loving Scarlett.

If Brady had these fears as the week went by, he didn't express them, and Libby didn't need any encouragement to keep her thoughts and feelings to herself. They were safer inside her. She'd learned that. They were less real, and not open to argument or disdain.

When Brady casually set the girls up in the living room together before their evening meal, with toys to play with, or encouraged Colleen to sit in the crook of one arm while Scarlett snuggled in the other and listened to him read a story, Libby had to fight her emotions back, fight the urge to grab Colleen and take her into another room.

She was careful not to let her conflicted feelings show.

I wonder if she's cooking, Brady thought, sitting back in his black leather swivel chair late on Friday afternoon.

Libby had cooked all week. Monday, some kind of pork chop thing in a rich gravy, with mashed potatoes, parsleyed carrots and string beans. Tuesday, grilled fish with French fries and salad. Wednesday, chicken pot pie, and Thursday, an Oriental fried rice.

His stomach rumbled, just as Gretchen knocked on his open office door and marched across his almost-new carpet. "Are you busy, Brady?"

No, just fantasizing about dinner.

"What is it, Gretchen?"

One look at her face and he knew.

Resignation day.

And she didn't just hand him the letter, she wanted to talk. "I'm sorry it's not working out for you," he said when she finished, leaning forward and letting his palms fall heavily onto the desk.

He hoped she'd pick up on the signals he was sending. He felt for her, and didn't want to lose her, but wasn't sure what more she wanted, or what he could give. At that moment, there was a click as the outer office door opened and Nate appeared. Inwardly, Brady swore.

"Glad I caught you, boss," Nate said, striding forward. He had a long envelope in his hand, and a "man's gotta do what a man's gotta do" look on his face that Brady immediately didn't want to see there.

Then Nate caught sight of Gretchen. "Oh," he said. *Oh,* spelled like a four-letter word. He dropped the envelope on Brady's desk and shuffled back, dropping his voice to a fast and almost incomprehensible mumble. "Letter of resignation. Four weeks notice. Count on you as a reference? See you Monday."

Gretchen sat with a stony stare on her face. Nate's dark flush had reached halfway up his face. Brady stood up. "Now, hang on a minute, guys, there's no need for you *both* to go."

He realized as soon as he'd said it what a hole he'd dug himself into.

By the time he got home an hour and a half later, after picking up Scarlett from his mom's, he was more than ready for an easy night. He wanted a night that included Libby's cooking, but somehow managed *not* to include her turbulent effect on his senses. He wanted a night when Colleen would be a playmate for Scarlett because they'd started to get cute together over the past couple of days, but with no nagging perception that he and Libby still weren't doing it right.

He got the home cooking, at least.

Libby had made a big pot of chicken and corn chowder. The stove was off but the pot was still piping hot, and the aroma reached out to him as soon as he opened the door. It pulled him in, eased the tension in his neck and practically said to him, "Can I take off your coat, pour you a beer and massage your shoulders?"

"Hundwy," Scarlett said, smelling it, too.

"Yeah, me, too, sweetheart," he answered. He listened. The house was very quiet, and there was only the one light on in the kitchen. "I wonder where your—" He stopped.

This was one of the things they just couldn't get their heads around. Was Libby ''your mommy''? Logically, since the girls were twins, she had to be, but they'd both agreed that it didn't feel right yet. Libby almost seemed scared about it, although she never said so.

At the moment, he couldn't envisage how it ever would feel right, and it left him with these abrupt pauses in his conversations with Scarlett, when he reached a crossroads and didn't know whether to go left to ''Mommy'' or right to ''Colleen's mom'' or straight ahead and just say ''Libby.''

They'd had separate timetables all this week, running through different routines each morning and not meeting up until late afternoon. The girls only got to see each other for an hour or two, and though that was probably good—you couldn't rush it, you couldn't force the connection—it felt weird, too.

Brady wasn't particularly happy about having Scarlett in day care forty hours a week, but he didn't have a choice. Meanwhile, Colleen got to be with her mom for all those extra hours. At heart, he believed in working it like that. Where possible, little kids should spend their time in the care of someone who loved them. But this wasn't a perfect world, and Scarlett could only have that for three days a week.

Libby was so great around the house, and such a great mom, it was tempting to try for the whole package. She could look after both girls, keep the place nice and make more of those mouth-watering meals. They could put Scarlett and Colleen in a part-time preschool program so she could have some time to herself. Maybe she'd like to take a class or just shop and drink coffee, once she had some friends. He'd cover her expenses, if she wanted. Once she and Colleen moved out, he'd employ her as a nanny, or—or—

Yeah, right, and maybe he'd get a fifties haircut, a black-and-white TV, and a white picket fence for the front yard, while he was at it! This situation wasn't 1950s clear-and-simple, and couldn't ever be. At least he'd had sense enough not to mention the idea of splitting their roles to her. And after the fiasco this afternoon with Gretchen and Nate, he wasn't planning on messing with gender equity issues for a while.

Right now, he just wanted some of that soup.

"Libby?" he called.

No answer. It didn't look like she was home. Then he saw a light seeping from under the door down to the basement, so he opened it and called down, but again there was no reply. He smelled something above the seductive curls of steam from the soup. It was an odor of burning plastic, and it came from the basement.

Grabbing Scarlett in his arms, he hurried down, concerned. Scarlett liked it down here, fortunately. He'd painted the cement floor in heavy-duty pale gray paint, and set up half the space as a play area for her, with a piece of thick carpet, a slide, a green plastic alligator rocker and a toy kitchen set. Scarlett went to play on the slide right away, leaving Brady to assess the scene.

The dryer door was open, revealing a damp pile of clothing sitting in the bottom of the tumbler, and the smell he'd detected was coming from the machine's air vent at the back. The motor had apparently gotten burned out. He looked around. There was hand washing pegged on a nylon rope strung near the furnace.

Her underwear.

Okay.

He tried not to look at it. It wasn't relevant.

The dryer motor was burned out. Libby wasn't here. He was getting lightheaded from hunger. Those things were relevant. Her underwear wasn't. Should he be concerned that she wasn't here? Had she called anyone about the dryer? Should he look for a note she might have left? And should he feed Scarlett, who would soon be as hungry as he was?

For the moment, she was still happy on the slide, and he moved a little closer to the underwear. Maybe he should hang up the wet stuff from the dryer? Would it fit on the line? It was a little hard to check the available space without getting pretty familiar with what was already on it.

"Who am I kidding here?" Brady groaned aloud.

"Daddy, Daddy, Daddy," Scarlett said.

"Yeah, I know. This isn't right," he answered her, but he kept looking all the same.

So this was Libby's underwear...

She didn't go for brief, but she went for sheer. He saw net and lace and thin, almost transparent silk, in the same pastels and creams and whites she favored in her outer clothing. Soft bra cups, frilly edgings, little ribbons tied into bows.

He groaned again.

Upstairs, seconds later, he heard a door slam shut and toddling footsteps. He flinched with guilt and called gruffly at once, "Libby, is that you?" He stepped back toward the dryer, away from what he'd really been looking at.

"Oh, you found it, didn't you?"

Yes, and it's better than a lingerie catalogue.

"I'm so sorry, it's my fault," she went on. "I'll pay for the repair, or for a new machine."

"The dryer." Right. Right. "Yeah, I could smell it." She was coming down the stairs. "It wasn't your fault," he said. "It's pretty old."

She appeared, carrying Colleen. They must have been out for a walk, or something. They both had pink cheeks and red noses and bright eyes.

"No, you see, I forgot to empty the lint filter before I started," she said. She put Colleen down, slid out the filter and showed it to him. The curved screen of wire was coated in a soft, thick felt of gray-blue the approximate color of his towels. She peeled it off. "See? The air couldn't get through, or something."

"No, the motor was old. It's okay. Hey, I'm glad there's a household task you're not perfect at, Libby. I always forget to empty the lint filter, too."

"I kind of like it when it gets thick." She wrinkled up her nose. " Because then it peels off so nicely, in one long strip." She frowned, clapped her hands to her pink cheeks. "That's pretty weird, isn't it?" She seemed surprised at herself, oddly in awe. "I've never told that to anyone before—that I have a thing about dryer lint."

"I won't blackmail you with it."

"That's what you'd say, though, isn't it?" Her cheeks were still pink, but she'd relaxed now, and seemed a little giddy. "At first? The escalating demands for cash would come later."

He laughed, feeling the tightness in his neck and temples ease. She'd confessed about her lint fetish, maybe he should confess that he'd ogled her underwear.

Uh, no. Sins of a different size.

"I'll check it out later, see if we need a new motor or a new machine," he said instead. "When this furnace is on, things dry pretty fast down here anyhow." They both looked toward her underwear, and looked quickly away again. "The soup smells great," he added quickly.

"Colleen and I walked down to the store to get some good bread to go with it. We can eat whenever you want."

"Now?" He couldn't keep the hunger out of his voice, and explained, "I'm wiped. I had two of my best people try to resign today. When I stupidly tried to argue that, since they were resigning because of each other, only one of them really had to go, I had both of them telling me, 'So, choose!' It was horrible. My office manager cried. My site manager stormed out. One minute I'm a sexist pig, the next I'm a sucker for a female sobbing act. As the situation stands, neither of them are speaking to me."

"And you lost both of them?"

"Yeah. I couldn't choose. I mean, I *couldn't*."

"You need more than soup."

"What else are you offering?"

Hell, don't make it sound so suggestive, Brady!

"Chocolate cake with almond vanilla ice cream and hot fudge sauce." She led the way upstairs, her bottom swaying like a dancing peach.

"Don't move out, Libby," he said, sounding too much as if he meant it.

She laughed, then sobered. "Yeah, well, we're not, as of this afternoon."

"You haven't found anywhere?"

"I've found lots of places I don't like. You know, they win on several optional criteria, like having a park in easy distance, or being on a quiet street, then they hit one big, fat deal-breaker. Too expensive. Too small. Pathological landlord."

She gave a short laugh, but her face was really tight, now, and her shoulders were tense. His hungry stomach sank. All joking aside, she was seriously anxious to leave, and he was a heel for thinking she should stay just because it was convenient for him, coming home to such great meals and warm company—*and such erotic underwear*—after a hard day.

He felt—and this was crazy and without foundation—as if he'd been slapped in the face.

He shut the door to keep the girls safe from the steep, backless basement stairs, and tried to regain some ground. "I talked to the manager at Scarlett's day care today, and she wants to meet you, sometime late next week if that works for you. They're looking for someone in their part-timers' room."

"I liked the casual-care room there," she answered slowly. She'd left Colleen there for the first time just this afternoon, although the option had been available all week. "I liked the atmosphere of the center as a whole."

"You know, we could work something out with you taking care of Scarlett outside those hours, too."

Again, she frowned. "I need more than part-time."

"Talk to the manager. I agree it's a nice place. I'm sure we can work something out."

Libby knew where Brady kept all his dishes by this time. She got out two deep china bowls for them and two shallow plastic bowls for the girls, hoping Brady wouldn't see how tense she was. She'd made the soup to soothe her own emotions, not his.

She hadn't been joking when she'd mentioned pathological landlords, but didn't want to relive an unpleasant experience by talking about it. Didn't want to risk the wrong reaction from Brady, either.

As well, she'd been to a promising job interview today, at a place called the Toyland Children's Center, and had been offered the position. She'd asked for the weekend to think it over.

The hours were longer than she wanted—forty-five hours a week, Monday through Friday, with one hour off in the middle for lunch—and although the place wasn't terrible by any means, it wasn't as nice as the day-care center she'd worked in back in Minnesota. The toys were older and less varied. The playground was smaller and less sheltered. It was a step down for Colleen.

And now here was Brady making plans for her without asking in advance.

She hadn't known he intended to mention her job search at Scarlett's day care. He meant well, she was sure of that, but she reacted against it all the same. She didn't want him organizing her life, making her decisions. She definitely didn't want to depend on him financially.

He'd taken out a cutting board and a serrated knife and was cutting the bread with a smooth, easy action, like a carpenter cutting wood. The slices peeled off thick and straight. Libby brought the soup to the table and ladled it into the bowls. It was a one-pot meal— her mother's recipe, thick with corn, potato, chicken, celery, carrots and cream.

They ate largely in silence, using the girls to deflect the usual awkwardness. Colleen and Scarlett
were tired at the end of a long week, and both began
to droop while still in their high chairs.

Separately, Libby and Brady carried each child upstairs. In separate bathrooms, they brushed their
teeth. In separate bedrooms, they got them into night-
time diapers and fluffy sleepsuits, and tucked them
into their cribs. They were both ready to come down
again at exactly the same time.

"I think they're starting to get in sync with each
other," Brady said. "Did you notice they woke up
within five minutes of each other this morning? Neither of them finished their soup, both of them ate all
their bread, and they both started crying with tired-
ness at the same time." He cleared his throat.
"They're a lot more in sync than we are."

"What are you saying, Brady?"

"Just that having them mesh together might make
things easier than we think, when we're living separately and arranging playdates and sleepovers."

"Is that what we're going to do? Sleepovers?"

"Isn't it?"

"I guess."

"We wanted to bring the girls together," he reminded her.

It was the divorce-without-the-marriage thing that
Libby's friends had lamented over, on her behalf.
They'd been right. She didn't want it. The idea of
losing Colleen for two nights every second weekend,
even though it meant gaining Scarlett for the other
weekends, made her feel empty and scared. She was
used to herself and Colleen being a team of two, and
almost never being apart. She wasn't used to won-

dering what twin daughters were doing, out of her care.

"You look tired, Brady," she said, avoiding a real answer, and hoping he wouldn't notice she'd avoided an agreement as well. "I'll clean up tonight, if you want to sit." He'd stacked the dishwasher all this week, since she'd cooked.

He looked at her for a moment, as if weighing his options, then shook his head. "Thanks. I don't need to sit. I'm going to take a look at that dryer." He disappeared down to the basement.

The kitchen was warm. Without thinking about what she was doing, Libby took off her sweater and laid it over the back of Colleen's highchair and started clearing up. As she worked, her thoughts skittered along like a sewing machine, basting her plans together like basting temporary seams, using big, makeshift stitches.

I'll take that full-time job, if it's offered, and if nothing better comes up next week. I'll go see the manager at Scarlett's day-care center, just so I can tell Brady I did it, but I won't take a part-time job. Hopefully, we can get past the problem of his suggestion without having a confrontation. I'll just tell him it didn't work out. I don't want him organizing my life. I don't want him even *thinking* about it!

Brady wasn't in the basement for long. He unplugged the power cord, opened the back of the dryer and found the motor. It was definitely burned out, and he thought it probably wasn't worth replacing or trying to fix. He screwed the back of the dryer into place again, listening to the occasional creak of the floorboards over his head as Libby moved around in the kitchen upstairs.

It frustrated him that she frequently wouldn't spill what was on her mind. All that "It's fine" stuff. It angered him occasionally, but at the same time he didn't want to crowd her, or push her to talk. His instinct was to respect the signals she sent out, to give her space. For now, at least.

Words were slippery little beasts, in any case. Two people could talk and talk and end up saying nothing...especially if one of them was lying. You could listen to someone pouring their heart out, and take it all seriously, lose half a night of sleep over it, and the next day it would turn out to be, quote unquote, "just a mood." He didn't want to get into all that again.

He twisted the last screw tight into the dryer back, put the screwdriver away and went upstairs again. Libby was at the sink, with her back to him, and he felt his gut shift and his blood beat at the sight of her.

Her hair was twisted up in a clip so he could see the curve at the back of her neck. He immediately started to imagine how it would smell. Her back stretched a little to the side as she reached for the empty soup pot. He should have guessed she'd scorn to put cooking pots in the dishwasher. She was a woman with standards.

Standards, and the softest, prettiest figure he'd seen in months.

"Any good news on the dryer?" she asked, half turning and half smiling, so that the ceiling light contoured her face, her breasts and her hips. His blood beat harder.

"No, it's dead," he said, struggling to keep even the pretense of focus. "Guess I'm going shopping for a new one—" He stopped.

She'd taken her sweater off, and he could see the baby-soft stretches of skin on the inner curves of her arms. Streaking diagonally down one of them was a long, ugly red scratch that had to be only a few hours old.

She realized he'd seen it before he said anything, and if he'd thought there might have been an innocent explanation, that thought evaporated as soon as he saw her hunted expression. This was something she hadn't wanted to tell him about, and wouldn't have, if he hadn't seen it.

He couldn't imagine why she'd feel this way, but he'd already let enough of her silences and evasions slip past without challenge this week. Hell, he hated this stuff!

"—weekend," he finished, then added without drawing breath, "What happened to your arm?" He made quite sure that she knew he was angry.

"I'm fine. It's okay. It's not deep. It's nothing." Stupid to say it. Libby knew she'd have to explain the whole event now that he'd seen the scratch, now that he'd asked so directly.

"That's not what I asked," Brady said.

Okay.

She took a breath. "I just had a sleazy experience with a landlord today, that's all. It wasn't a big deal."

Not that she'd felt quite this calm about it at the time. She'd felt repelled, and caught off guard.

"Tell me." His eyes were bright and hard.

She tried to make light of it. "It wasn't a partic-

ularly nice place. A duplex—half-double—over toward Indianola. Handsome landlord thought that the
prospect of his sexual services might prove an added
inducement to my taking the place. I communicated
that he was mistaken. He attempted a more seductive
form of persuasion.''

''Sweet jiminy! And you didn't *tell* me?''

''I am telling you. I'm telling you now.''

''You weren't going to.''

He was right. She'd dreaded having to talk about
it, experiencing a familiar, stomach-caving reluctance that she never fully understood in herself. Why
did she so hate to share important emotions? Why
did she so rarely ask for emotional support? Why did
she keep these kinds of things locked inside her
whenever she could?

Glenn had been a good, steady man. Just because
he hadn't listened to her particularly well, just because he'd controlled too many of their decisions and
had taken all her agreements for granted…that
wasn't an explanation. She'd actively *wanted* all that
when she'd fallen in love with him at nineteen. He'd
never been abusive or cruel. She'd wanted her rock-
like certainty that he'd always be there, strong and
sure of his needs and hers, and in that way she'd
chosen well. He always had been.

The independence she'd built since Glenn's death
had done a lot to cancel out the bad patterns that had
grown up in their marriage, but it hadn't gotten rid
of this sickening dread of laying out her emotions or
admitting to her needs in front of someone important.

And now Brady was angry because she'd said
nothing about today's experience.

''You wouldn't have told me,'' he went on, his

face tight and dark, "if I hadn't seen that ugly scratch on your arm."

"I guess not," she said. It was inadequate, and she knew it.

"Why? I hate that." His low voice had a rough note in it. "I hate lies and evasions."

"I never lied."

"Silence is a kind of lying, isn't it?" His eyes were narrowed and bright.

"Is it?" The idea shocked her. She didn't think of herself as someone who lied.

"Hell, I wish I'd been there!" He paced the kitchen. "You shouldn't have had to deal with something like that! You were looking at a house, not cruising a bar!"

"I guess this is why—one reason—why I didn't want to tell you," she said. She was almost stammering, trying to understand what was going on inside herself, and she could feel the fire in her cheeks. "Because there's nothing you can say or do, and it only makes two of us feel bad." This wasn't the whole of it, though. She knew that.

"What did you do when it happened?" he asked, his whole body still angular and distant.

"I kneed him and ran out."

"Where?"

"Just into the street, to my car. The whole thing only lasted thirty seconds."

"I mean where did you knee him?"

"There's only one place to knee a man, Brady," she said impatiently, and somehow, suddenly, it was almost funny, in a black sort of way.

"And you kneed him *there?*" A slow grin, an impressed grin, was breaking onto his face.

"Didn't I just tell you that? Oh, lord!" She covered her face with her hands for a moment, then looked up at him again. "I was just glad I didn't have Colleen with me! I went straight over and picked her up. Just *hugged* her."

Brady muttered something, and covered the distance between them before she could draw breath. He ran his hands lightly up her arm, exploring the swollen scratch with incredibly gentle fingertips, setting every fine hair on end.

"Sweet jiminy!" he muttered again. "You were upset. You still are. You don't want to pursue this, Libby?"

"No." She shook her head. "I want to forget it. The scratch only came when I wrenched myself free. He was wearing a chain bracelet. I guess it must have had a half-open link with a sharp end. He wasn't trying to hurt me. He was just a good-looking sleaze who doesn't get told no often enough. The kneeing him thing was probably over the top on my part."

"The kneeing him thing was great." Brady's arms were light and soft around her—supporting her but ready to drop if she didn't want them. She did want them, as it happened—far too much. "I'm impressed," he said.

"Not that I'm pleased about that, or curious or anything, but...why?"

"It's not a big target, the place where you knee a man."

"You would have expected me to miss?"

"To be honest, yes. You keep surprising me, Libby." His voice had softened, and he wasn't trying, anymore, to keep the smile off his face. He was letting her see it, confident of her response.

"We've only known each other for around six weeks," she answered, smiling but still a little shaky. Getting shakier, actually, with his touch and his warmth surrounding her. It was a different kind of shaky. Nice. Amazingly nice. "We've been living under the same roof for just seven days. I should hope I'm still surprising you."

"Yeah, but I have a feeling you'll go on doing it for a while."

"It might be fun, surprising you."

He still hadn't let her go. He held her lightly, his body motionless, and she didn't move away. They looked into each other's faces, suspended in the expectant, important moment. Libby hadn't seen him this close before. But she'd wanted to, for days. His eyes were steady and open and serious and warm. His mouth was still and closed, imperfectly shaped with the tiny scar that nicked his upper lip, but perfectly kissable.

She wanted to kiss it. Softly at first, just to see how it felt, then a little deeper if it felt good, which every intuition and every nerve-ending in her body told her it would. His mouth was a magnet, with its own energy field. Her senses were mixed up, plugged into the wrong outlets. The scent of him drowned out her hearing, and his whispered words blinded her to sight.

She reached up and touched the tips of her fingers to his lips, and her mouth was only a few inches farther away. Dropping her fingers lower, she placed them softly in the curve between his neck and his shoulder.

Brady moved even closer. His thighs dragged against her skirt, two hard columns of warmth. He dropped the cradling touch on her bare arms and brushed his hands down her sides, nudging the swell of her breasts in passing and at once making them tingle and grow full with need. Her pulses slowed, and there was an aching heaviness in her core.

"What will you do if I kiss you?" he whispered, letting his palms come to rest against the curves of her hips. His mouth was an inch from hers—so close, but still not close enough. Her whole body ached with the exquisite torture of wanting that tiny space to disappear. "I know you won't turn away, Libby. I know it."

"No, I won't turn away...." She lifted her face to meet the soft brush of his lips.

Chapter Six

Their mouths pouted and opened, making the kiss full and deep almost at once. Her breasts pushed against his chest. She felt the roughness of prickly new beard on his jaw, as necessary to her senses as salt on an egg, and tasted cool mint and cinnamon in his mouth. Time melted and stretched.

The air around them was sweet and silent, and the kitchen lighting was yellow and warm. Upstairs, the girls slept at opposite ends of the house, not yet fully sisters, but under the same roof, beloved and safe.

"I've wanted to do this since I met you," Brady said. He held her face between his hands and stole another kiss from her mouth, and then another. His eyes, blurred with need, learned her face by heart.

"It isn't that long ago," she answered. Couldn't even think, at the moment. Felt like hours...or like months. It wasn't *relevant,* somehow. She touched him, hips and back and thighs, loving the hard warmth and the solid strength that her eager hands found.

"Seems longer," he said. "Seems…intense, you know, important, the time we've known each other."

"It has been, Brady." She rested her cheek against his chest, listening to his heartbeat, feeling the weight of his arms around her. "In a lot of ways, we jumped in at the deep end, because of the girls. I've tried—"

"Not to. I know." He kissed her hair and her temples, coaxing her to give him her mouth once more. She didn't want to give it yet. She still needed the sound of his breathing, and his heart. Instead, she cupped her hand against his jaw and he began to kiss her palm, his lips soft and deliberately erotic, sending thrills chasing up her arm and radiating through her body. "We've tried to hold back," he said. "To take this sensibly and carefully, but we didn't anticipate—"

"Yes. That it would be so hard. I keep wondering if it's like stirring up a pond with a big stick. The water gets cloudy, and you don't know what's really there."

The words came spilling out, giving her vertigo. It was terrifying to talk this way, even when she hid behind obscure comparisons with muddy ponds. She took a breath, steeling herself to force out the starker questions, the ones closer to her heart. She couldn't even look at him. She just needed the warm wall of his chest to lean on.

"Are we just feeling like this because our daughters are twins?" she said. "Are we just trying to find a way for us to fit together because we want the girls to? Is it all *wishful,* not real?"

There was a long beat of silence.

"That's too complicated, isn't it?" he said slowly, at last.

It probably was. He was right.

Stop talking, Libby. Keep it to yourself. Safe inside.

Nothing about this felt complicated tonight. It felt simple. A man and a woman, and chemistry so strong it was like a physical entity, a thick, magical webbing woven around them, a sorcerer's spell.

"Way too complicated," he repeated. He brushed the hair back from her forehead, then tilted her chin upward in his cupped hand and softened his mouth against hers once more.

It was so good. She wanted to disappear into the blind darkness of it for hours, without thinking, without feeling anything but this. She wanted his strength, his simple certainties, his casual generosity of spirit.

All of these qualities were contained in the way he was touching her. Arms wrapped around her, body shored against hers, hard and male. Mouth giving, and giving again, pressing against her temples, her hair, her jaw, her neck. Hands exulting in the texture of her clothing and her skin, finding sensations that made him shudder and gasp against her mouth.

He touched her breasts as if he already knew them, as if he'd wanted them forever, and had explored them in his dreams. He found the gap between top and skirt at her waist and slid his hands inside and up, cupping her, thumbing her nipples, lifting the weight of her breasts and bending his face to hold his hot mouth against them through the fabric of her clothing.

Sensation ran over her like trickles of ice and fire, and she throbbed inside. She couldn't open her eyes. Just couldn't. They were so heavy with need. Her body whipped and twisted against him and she had to cling to him for balance, to keep them both anchored to the earth.

"Libby, tell me to stop!" he whispered at last, after minutes...or maybe years.

"Stop," she said obediently, then, fierily honest, "No, don't! Please don't!"

"I want to take you upstairs."

"I like upstairs."

"To bed."

"I know. I know, Brady."

He pulled away. "How can I do this?"

She read the appeal in his face. He was asking her to help him save them both from this, in case it was a huge mistake. "How can you *not?*" she answered him. "Even if we stop, can we really go back?"

"Less of a distance to travel back from just a kiss than from making love to you all night."

It was a blunt statement, Brady realized, as soon as he'd said it.

But he wasn't sorry.

It had to be said.

He couldn't believe how good Libby felt in his arms, how lost in this and how giving she'd been. No games, no pretense, no hidden agenda, no secondary goals that she wanted to leverage with sex, the way Stacey always had.

He wasn't used to this. It was new, and it added hugely to the intensity of what he felt himself. Libby's blind responsiveness had pulled him close to breaking point with a speed and power that left him breathless and trembling, and the only reason he was holding back now, after that forever-long kiss, was because of *her,* because *she* might regret it, or blame him for it, or get caught in the net of its complexities.

He was sure that he wouldn't. And anyhow, he didn't care. He had the dizzy, heart-pounding confidence and carelessness of a man aching and throbbing and desperate for release, and there was just one tiny little part of his mind that had sense enough to know that he might not always feel this way, and that Libby almost certainly wouldn't.

So he'd said it, and now he needed her to help, to agree, to take the ball and run with it or, so help him, it would be too late.

"Yes, okay. Yes." She stepped back.

Damn!

A shudder rippled through her body. She sniffed, smoothed her skirt, tried to smile. "Yes," she said again. "Thanks for that—uh—timely reminder. I'm sorry."

"Sorry?" His voice hurt his throat. "Lord, Libby, don't be *sorry.* It wasn't your fault."

"I shouldn't have needed you to talk sense into me."

"I shouldn't have been so good at it!" he muttered.

She laughed. "Is that some kind of no-means-yes scenario?"

"Could have been," he admitted. "I could…uh… probably still appreciate a really powerful argument from you about why I'm wrong, and why it's more than okay for us to go upstairs and— If you've got one?" he added hopefully.

She laughed again. Nervous. Shaken up by what

had happened. He recognized how rocked she was by the intensity of what she'd felt.

"I don't think I do," she said. "I think you were right. If nothing else, we need to sleep on this. Oh, bad word choice! I mean, we need to *examine* this, in a cooler light, and...probably...as you said... travel back."

"Maybe one of us should travel upstairs and take a cold shower."

"I'm going to go look at the girls," Libby said. "They're my compass. They keep me pointing steady."

"Let me finish here, then," Brady answered. There were still the bench tops to be wiped. That had to be almost equivalent to a cold shower. "I'm imagining myself following you up the stairs and it...uh...leads to other ideas."

"Mm." Libby didn't want to admit that she found it all too easy to picture those ideas for herself, and backed out of the room quickly while she still had a chance of covering the distance.

At the top of the stairs, she paused for a moment. Everything was quiet. No sounds from either of the girls. Brady always checked on Scarlett last thing before he went to bed, and there was no real need for her to do so. Still, for some reason she found her feet carrying her in the direction of Scarlett's room, where she tiptoed to lean over the crib.

Fast asleep. On her chest and her knees, with her head turned to one side and her bottom stuck up in the air. Colleen often slept the same way. It looked deeply uncomfortable, but apparently it wasn't. Scarlett's little quilt had come off, too. Libby tucked it around her shoulders again, over that hump of a bottom, and stroked her dark curls.

She heard the whispered words fall from her mouth almost before she knew she was going to say them. "I love you, Scarlett."

Then she clung to the side of the crib until the strength came back into her legs, because she was so scared of the weight of her own feelings, so scared of how much power the future had to hurt her now.

"I'm going to head straight out after breakfast to shop for a new dryer," Brady said. "If you want to come. Thought we could see if we can pick up a Vietnamese cookbook, too, and some ingredients."

They'd all slept in this morning, and Brady and Libby had been lazy with their routine, getting the girls dressed and fed. It was already almost 9:30.

"That would be fun," Libby answered.

Fun, and like walking on a knife blade, the way she was feeling this morning. Brady hadn't touched her, and his smile had snapped on and off as if activated by a switch. When she poured two mugs of coffee, he stood back out of the way until she'd taken hers and moved out of range. Out of touching range. Out of body-heat range.

She hadn't expected to see so much regret in his body language, so much stiff-as-cardboard caution in the way he moved. He really wasn't planning to let the electricity back into the air, today.

Even the innocent presence of the girls couldn't drain the tension away. Every time Libby looked at Scarlett, and when she picked her up to put her in the high chair, or lifted Scarlett's bib and used it to wipe the messy cereal from around her little mouth, she thought of what Brady had said about "traveling back."

Everything you did for a child took you farther down the road toward feeling like a mother, toward *loving* like a mother, and Libby didn't see how you could ever travel back from that. She was stuck. The rock and the hard place. She wanted to give Colleen a full and loving relationship with her twin, and yet she wanted to keep her own distance, to protect herself from loss, even while knowing it was already too late. Loving one twin meant loving the other, and she already did.

As for Brady...

Her heart and her stomach both flipped. Organs shouldn't behave like acrobats. And a mouth shouldn't have such a good memory. So they'd kissed. They'd acted on the chemistry. And they'd both agreed it was a bad idea. She should be grateful that he apparently wasn't finding it as hard as she was to forget just how good and right it had felt between them last night.

Why was it so hard for her? Why did her mouth taste him again, feel him again, purely because they both happened to put their lips to the rims of their coffee mugs at the same time? Why did even one of those short, blink-on-and-blink-off-again smiles of his arrow straight to her heart?

She wasn't used to this chemistry. That was part of it. Her feelings for Glenn hadn't begun this way. She'd needed him for other reasons, seeing him as mature and successful and grounded, someone who wouldn't let her down.

In fact, Glenn's sexual hunger had been too much for her at first. She'd been aware of him trying to

rein it in, to control himself at each stage of their
growing intimacy, to go slowly for her sake. He
hadn't asked her if that was what she'd needed or
wanted, he'd made the decision himself.

And he'd consciously taught her. "Feel this, Lisa-
Belle. This is what happens to a man."

And strangely, his attempts to educate her, to romance her with lavish gestures and to go slow with
her had had the opposite effect to the one he'd intended. She'd gotten more intimidated about sex, not
less. She hadn't felt able to put her needs and her
feelings into words. It had taken them a while to get
it right.

With Brady, in contrast, she felt like a floodgate
was about to break open.

As agreed, they took the girls to the mall after
breakfast and shopped for a new dryer, as serious as
a bridal couple choosing their silverware pattern, but
not nearly as physical. No stolen honeymoon kisses,
no special looks. But the salesman assumed they
were a couple, of course, and two people couldn't
look at the same dryer without standing pretty close,
even when they had two little girls in strollers to get
in the way.

Brady made the final choice about the dryer, and
arranged for the new machine to be delivered later
that afternoon. Next, they went to a bookstore and
found a South-East Asian cookbook with a section
of recipes from Vietnam. They sat in the mall's food
court and had some lunch, looking through the cookbook for a couple of recipes to try tonight.

The book itself looked almost good enough to eat,
filled with gorgeous colour photographs of steaming
hot dishes, garnished with glossy red chillies or

bright green sprigs of coriander. Brady shifted his chair closer to Libby's and slid the book across so that they could both look at it together, and his arm brushed hers as he turned a page.

She didn't move away. Couldn't. Felt her body lean closer without consciously making it happen. His arm pressed against hers. Her insides crumbled, and she heard Brady let out a jerky breath.

"Damn it, Libby," he muttered, and his hand closed over hers. He turned a little, took the hand away again and wrapped his fingers tightly over the back of her chair, then looked into her face with suffering eyes and said, "Help me, here. I've been fighting all morning, and I'm *aching* now. Don't make me do all the work!"

Was *that* what his rigid distance had meant? She felt a sweet wash of relief that she knew was totally unwarranted. Okay, so they were on the same page, but it was blank, Wasn't it? They'd agreed to leave it that way.

"Rice paper rolls," she answered, gabbling. "How about that? And beef with lemongrass. The girls have finished their lunch. We can go. If that's what you want."

"Hell, it's not what I want," he said. "It's painfully obvious what I want, and you know it, but we've talked about it, we've agreed, so, yeah…yeah, let's do that."

There were several Oriental grocery stores along High Street, so as well as taking a detour through the supermarket, they stopped at one on the way home and shopped for the ingredients they needed, getting some advice from the pretty young woman at the register.

"What adorable little girls you have!" she said.

"She's being tactful," Brady murmured to Libby. "They're not being adorable right now."

Since it was midafternoon by this time, Colleen and Scarlett had had enough of shopping, and were ready to go home. Freed from their strollers, they toddled around with busy, curious hands, eager to pull the unfamiliar items off the shelves. It took their parents twice as long as it should have done to find everything they needed.

The twins were tired by the time Brady nosed his car into the garage.

"Shall we sit them on the couch with a music video and a couple of toys while we put away the food?" he suggested. "Then take them up for a late nap?"

"Sounds like a plan."

They put away the groceries together, careful in the same way they'd been careful this morning, giving each other too much space. Halfway through the task, the dryer arrived. Brady signed off on the delivery and helped the two men to get the new appliance into position in the basement. The toddler music video burbled away in the background, and Libby finally said, "I'll go check on the girls. They're being very quiet."

They were asleep together on the couch.

Libby saw two little shoulders pressed against each other, four fans of black lashes feathered against four pink, satiny cheeks, and eight little limbs lost in a sea of masculine gray and white cushions. Colleen stood out in her bright pink leggings and top, with their white ribbons and little white stars. Scarlett, in navy, almost looked like another cushion.

But their little faces were just the same, and when she bent closer, Libby discovered that they were breathing in unison. She heard two feather-soft sighs puff from two little noses, followed by two silent in-breaths, and saw two little chests rising.

She heard Brady behind her. "Hey…" he said.

"Yes, look," she whispered back. "Come and look." She held out her hand to him. "And listen. They're breathing together."

"Oh, wow! Oh, they are!"

He came forward and they both watched the girls and their synchronized breathing for a long time, without saying a word.

We should kiss, Libby thought. I *want* to. And he does. We're not going to. But it feels so wrong just to stand here. So close, but not daring to touch. Feeling like this, we should hold each other, and—

"We should cook," Brady said.

"We should," she agreed quickly. "While they're asleep."

It was fun. Something to do. Something to distract them and drain away the tension. The rice paper rolls were tricky, and Brady did better with them than Libby. He made a neat heap of ingredients, including shrimp, shredded cabbage and mint, in the middle of the stretchy circle of softened rice paper, and folded the whole thing into a neat, cylindrical package that stayed in shape.

"There you go," he said. "Vietnamese burrito."

Libby's effort, in contrast, was a lumpy mess. She knew she'd have a lot more success with the main dish, which was more like the cooking she did every day and less like a craft project. Brady sliced the green onions for her, and inhaled chili and lemon-grass with appreciation as he worked.

"I like this stuff," he said. "Reminds me of when we were there picking up Scarlett. My dad served there, too. He never talked about it much, but when he did, it was always about the flavors of the country. The smells and the sounds. The people. The rivers and the rice fields and the sea. He was protecting us, probably, from the stuff he didn't want us to think about. He was…great that way."

His voice had roughened a little, and he twirled a green onion in his fingers without even seeing it.

"You loved him a lot," Libby blurted. Her hands stilled over the meat she was cutting, and she immediately wished she hadn't said it.

"We were pretty close," he agreed, still twirling the green onion. "Only child, and all that. Only son."

"Yes, I wondered— Your mom seems to love kids so much, but she only had—"

"Oh, tell me about it! She tried, Lib, for years. Had I don't know how many miscarriages. Three or four in a row. Got to six months with another one, then lost it and couldn't get pregnant again."

"Oh, dear God!" She was close to tears at once, thinking about how it must have been for Delia, and for Brady's dad.

"Then Stacey's infertility was a body blow. That's one of the reasons Mom was so thrilled to hear about Colleen. She's hungry for another grandchild."

"Of course. Of course she is." Libby understood, and yet she felt possessive and protective, too, and was ashamed of herself. What did she think Mrs. Buchanan was going to do? Kidnap Scarlett's twin?

"When they get to know each other better..." she offered lamely, vaguely "...they can, uh, spend more time together."

"That would be great," he answered. "She'd love to have Scarlett and Colleen to herself sometimes."

"Sure. That'd be fine."

But not yet. When I feel safer.

She went back to cutting the meat, knew he was looking at her but pretended not to see. After a moment, he said, "Hey, shall I put on some music? Want coffee, or a beer?"

"Coffee would be good."

"If it's coffee, I want cookies, too."

"Yes, please!"

"Here you go." He reached into the pantry and took one of the new packets they'd bought at the supermarket this afternoon, tore it open, stretched across and stuck one in Libby's mouth while she washed her meaty hands. Turning away from the sink, she tried to crunch on the cookie without letting half of it drop, but it didn't work. Brady lunged and caught the falling piece on its way to the floor, then lobbed it into Libby's wet, clean hands.

"I'm not eating it now." She lobbed it back to him. "It's soggy, and it's going to taste of chili and onion."

"Fussy!" Brady took her throw with a backhand like a tennis pro and the traumatized piece of cookie ricocheted and landed in the sink, on a bed of discarded green onion roots and torn cabbage leaves. They laughed, and looked at each other, and the kiss they were both thinking about seemed so real that Libby could almost see it in the air.

Chapter Seven

Brady took Libby to the Ohio State versus Indiana game the following Saturday. Mainly this was because he had his friend Matt's season ticket as well as his own, since Matt was out of town, but also because his mother virtually corralled the girls in his backyard and pushed him and Libby out the door.

"Go on," she told them. "You're young. You can sit on those rock-hard seats and still walk the next day. Parenthood isn't like joining a monastery. Have some fun."

Brady wasn't sure if Mom had intercepted any of the vibes between himself and Libby. If she had, she'd been unusually tactful. If she hadn't, she was losing her touch.

Since it was Libby's first game, he wanted to do it properly, so he packed a backpack with a scarlet-and-gray plaid picnic blanket for them to fold and sit on, a vacuum flask filled with hot soup because it was cold and she might not want beer, and a few other things. They also made a lightning stop at one of the stores on Lane Avenue, opposite campus, so he could buy her a Buckeye sweatshirt, a cap and a scarf.

When they'd driven halfway back home again looking for a place to park, had stepped out into the cold air, and she'd put on the things he'd bought, she looked—he sighed between his teeth—yeah, cute. Pretty.

Be honest, now. She looked completely irresistible.

Of course.

Mom was wrong. In his and Libby's case, parenthood, and doing it right for the girls, was *exactly* like joining a monastery. Brady had been resisting the irresistible all week, running for miles in the park every morning, taking those useless cold showers, and it was killing him. They flirted a little, but they didn't touch. They laughed, and then laughing got dangerous—too nice and warm and close—so they stopped. They talked, but they didn't talk about *this*.

He felt as if he was being pulled apart. He ached with wanting the good things—not just the sex, but the laughter and the sharing. And then he thought of the other stuff. All the things he'd hated in his marriage. The emotional landmines and man-traps and mazes with no exit.

He'd never found a way of handling it. Had to be him, didn't it? His fault, or his lack of perception? He should have…what? Listened more? Understood Stacey better? Or should he have yelled? Laid down the law?

Instead, he'd felt paralyzed by it all, and he'd ended up turning his back, withdrawing from the contest, steering his own steady middle course, keeping to what he believed, because maybe if one of them did that, things would end up okay.

He'd never confronted Stacey. He'd stopped listening, stopped taking her seriously, put everything down to her need for games. It had shocked him, after her death, to discover the evidence of her infidelity. He hadn't thought she would have gone that far, and he'd wondered, could he have pulled her back if he'd handled the earlier stuff differently?

He didn't want to end up in a mess like that again: so much anger, so many doubts. He wanted to stay well clear. So why was he letting himself feel like this about Libby?

She'd been to a couple of job interviews during the week. She'd looked at some more apartments, and had seen one she liked, but it wasn't near any of the jobs. She'd called the manager at Scarlett's day-care center, but she hadn't been to see her yet. "Her schedule was tight," she'd told him. "We couldn't find a time." She hadn't sounded like there was any urgency, and he'd been disappointed—he wanted to get things settled, hated hanging fire like this—but he'd let it go. Again.

Bundled up in hats and jackets, they walked down to the game, feeling the excitement build as they got closer. Streams of fans were converging on the huge stadium, and the Lane Avenue lot was crammed with cars, and people having tail-gate parties. Ticketless fans prowled around, looking desperate. Didn't anyone have a seat to sell? Noise overflowed from the top of the stadium. The band was already playing.

"Wow!" Libby said when they got to their seats.

The atmosphere was pumped up, energized, loud. The seats were an ocean of red and gray. The band was precision-perfect in its moves, and the announcer's voice echoed up to the sky and bounced back off the clouds.

Brady spread out the blanket, sat down next to Libby and thought about what Mom had said on the subject of rock-hard seats. Yeah, she was right, they weren't great, and they were cold, even through the blanket. To keep warm, you needed old friends to josh with. Failing that, you needed—ah, hell!—you needed to snuggle up to the gorgeous woman sitting next to you in her matching team colors and you needed to kiss the heat back into your blood.

"Soup?" he said desperately.

"Mmm, yes."

"It's canned. Sorry." His tongue and his brain were both on strike. She shouldn't be smiling back at him like that, as if this was fun and he was the perfect host. He felt as suave and as erudite as a block of wood, and his libido was yelling louder than the fans.

"Lib?" he said roughly, watching her face and her mouth. She had pink cheeks and bright eyes and glossy lips. And she was sitting very close. Was it just because she was crowded by the very large guy on the far side of her?

No, it wasn't.

"Mm?" she answered.

His voice dropped, still sounded way too husky. "Do me a favor before the soup?"

"Kiss you?" she suggested softly.

He just closed his eyes and nodded, then felt the

soft, lingering press of her mouth. It went away too soon.

"It's okay," Libby said. Brady opened his eyes, and she was watching him, intent and warm and close. "I mean, it's cold, and we, uh, just seem to get into this kind of trouble when we're alone." Alone because, somehow, the other ninety-seven thousand fans in the stadium didn't count.

"What are we going to do about it?" he asked, letting the agony show in his voice.

"The not doing anything idea doesn't seem to have worked out, this past week, does it?"

"Not as such, no."

"In fact, I kind of almost feel…"

"Yeah, that it's worse."

He couldn't remember when the outcome of a Buckeye game had meant so little to him. Maybe never. Even last year, when he'd still been suffering anger and loss, and had been struggling to take care of a baby on his own, he'd cared about the games. He'd bundled Scarlett up in a baby backpack and brought her along, and talked to her about every play as if she could understand.

Today, he talked to Libby about the plays, but really it was just so he could look at her, watch her mouth move when she asked questions—sensible, interested questions, most of them. He liked the way she was so ready to be involved, the way she entered into the spirit of the whole event.

Took them a while to get home afterward. They didn't push to get out of the stadium. It didn't matter if other people got ahead. And then there was the long walk up to the car, which they took slowly. Like lovers.

Delia was eating at a friend's, so she left as soon
as they got home. Libby changed out of her fan gear
into something soft and pretty, giving him painful
fantasies about what she was probably wearing underneath. They fed the girls eggs and bacon and
toast, and ordered in some take-out Chinese for
themselves, and, hell, Brady hoped that Libby was
imagining like he was what would happen as soon
as they got the girls to bed.

"Night-night, little girl," Libby whispered to
Scarlett.

She was teetering on the brink of sleep already,
all warm and soft and content. Brady had laid her in
her crib a few minutes ago, while Libby was still
singing to Colleen. Now Colleen was asleep, and—
it was getting to be a habit now, something she did
every night—she had crept in to say good-night to
Colleen's sister.

"I love you." It still took courage to say it, still
made Libby's stomach drop with fear when she
thought about the vulnerability it gave her, but she
said it anyway, because it was true.

Then she turned and met Brady in the doorway.
She wasn't surprised to see him there, waiting for
her, and she went right into his arms.

This time, they both knew from the start that this
was more than a kiss, and that they weren't stopping.
They simply held each other at first, too over-
whelmed to move. With her head pillowed against
his strong chest, Libby felt the heavy, shuddering
movement of his breathing, and the solid weight of
his arms.

He waited, giving her time, holding himself back

on the slimmest off-chance that, even after the way they'd suffered through the game this afternoon, she might not say yes to this. For some reason, she didn't want him to think this way—to put himself through any more waiting and doubt—even for a moment, so she took the initiative, curved one arm around the back of his warm neck and pulled him down to her.

He groaned against her mouth, eyes closed, body trembling. They kissed for a long time, anchored to the spot, unable to gather the will to move. Then Scarlett made a laughing sound in her sleep and they froze, looking toward the dim shape of the crib on the far side of the room. She settled and stilled again.

"Let's go," Brady growled. He grabbed Libby's hand and pulled her next door to his own room. She hadn't even set foot in it until now.

And now I know why.

It was his personal space, intimate in a way that the rest of the house wasn't. Before this moment, it would have been an invasion of his privacy. Now it was a major milestone in their response to each other.

He didn't switch on the light, so the space was filled with thick shadows. Having glimpsed its interior through the open doorway on visits to Scarlett's bedroom, Libby already knew it was a masculine room. Tonight it seemed even more so.

The bed was king-sized and furnished with sheets and comforter in a pattern of navy, gray and brown. The two bedside lamps were plain and practical, with cream shades and round ceramic bases, and the tall-boy and dresser were massive antiques, with an antique mirror to match. The bed was unmade, although she knew the sheets were fresh from the wash just yesterday, and he muttered an apology about the untidiness even as he pulled her onto the rumpled surface.

She might have thought him clumsy, if she hadn't been just as clumsy herself. This wasn't lack of grace and finesse on his part, this was overpowering, urgent need, and she felt just the same. One reach and pull and toss, and his shirt was over his head and onto the floor. In the dim light, his chest was an expanse of shadowed contours, narrowing to the waistband of his jeans.

Libby reached for the buttons that ran down the front of her cotton-knit cardigan top, but Brady closed his big hand over her fingers and said, "No, let me do this."

She gave a breathless agreement that barely counted as speech, then watched as he slipped each button free, opening the top wider as he went and letting his hands trail across the cups of her bra. "Ah, Libby..." he muttered. When he had finished, she sat up and he slid the garment off her shoulders and down her arms, then buried his face between her breasts.

She fumbled for her bra clip, impatient with it, and let him slide the bra free from her shoulders, too. Her breasts weren't lavish, but they filled his cupped hands, incredibly sensitive to his touch. He slid beside her and brushed her hair back onto the pillow, then kissed her again, sweet and slow, with his fingers still teasing her breasts, making her peaked nipples ache and her insides writhe like snakes.

She reached for his hips, unfastened his jeans and pushed her hands inside, finding heat and hardness pressed against soft black cloth. He shuddered, and she dragged at the side seams of his jeans so that he was freed a little.

Her own skirt was twisted around her lower body. Brady found the zipper and left her wearing only her cream net-and-lace panties. "You don't know..." he said, then stopped.

"Mm, what don't I know?" She smiled.

"...what this does to me. Can't decide. Which is sexier? On or off? They're sheer, Libby, and I can see everything I want in this world."

He curved his palms over her bottom, caressing the soft texture of the fine-woven net, and pulled her to him so that the ridge of his arousal, still straining to escape his black briefs, was pressed against her swollen heat.

They were explosively ready for each other.

He rolled onto his back and discarded his briefs, and she went willingly to rest on top of him, lifting herself a little so that he could take her breasts, first in his hands and then in his mouth. She gasped at the hot, wet suction, and he intensified the pull of lips and tongue until the sensation was so powerful she had to push his mouth away.

"I can't wait, Libby." His voice was rough and jagged as splintered wood.

"I know," she said. His arousal nudged at the apex of her thighs, and she ached to give him entry. "I don't want you to."

She rolled away again and slid her underwear down her hips, while he grabbed a packet from the bedside drawer and ripped it open, sheathing himself fluidly. She held out her arms and he fell into them like a man come home from battle, his release already imminent.

"I'm rushing you," he groaned.

"You're not. Don't make me wait." Libby wanted him, slick and full inside her, heavy on top of her, hot against her skin, spilling her over the edge. And she wanted him now.

She splayed her hands across his back and closed her eyes, her breathing ragged and shallow. He slipped inside her, completing a perfect joining that seemed like a beginning and an ending at the same time.

"Oh, Libby," he said.

"Brady…" She kissed him, hungry for his taste, then opened her mouth and dragged her teeth across his shoulder, hard enough to skim the boundary between pleasure and pain. He shuddered.

They rocked and bucked and clawed, while time twisted and folded. They were centered together in the wild, dark storm they'd made for each other, clinging for dear life, crying out in astonished ecstasy at the power of their shared climax.

Even as it ebbed, it overtook them again, like the aftershocks of an earthquake. When they were finally still, holding each other, quite breathless, Brady pulled up the forgotten comforter draped at the bottom of the bed and covered them, and they were silent for a long time, just feeling each other breathe, listening to each other's hearts.

"Hello, you," Brady finally said.

"Hello, yourself."

"I'm not going to talk."

"No."

"I'm not going to say a million times that this was amazing."

"Okay."

"But it was amazing, Libby."

"I—I thought so, too. Did you, um, know it was going to happen when you met me in the doorway of Scarlett's room? Did you come looking for me?"

"What do you think? Could have pretended, I guess, that I was checking she hadn't kicked off her covers."

"She had. I tucked them back."

"Thanks."

He lifted himself onto one elbow and looked at her, touched his fingertip to her nose, and to her lips. Then he replaced the finger with his mouth. It was a kiss like a ripe berry—small and juicy and sweet, but soon it grew.

He touched her breasts, lightly and gently at first, as if afraid that they might still be too tender from before. They weren't. She wanted this delectable friction across each hardened nipple, and she wanted his mouth—the hot caress of his breath, the pull of his lips and tongue as he drew those throbbing crests into his mouth and suckled her.

She writhed at every touch, and he whispered, "I love the way you can't keep still. Watch me try to make you stay in one spot."

He lifted her arms over her head and anchored her wrists to the pillow with the press of one forearm. His other hand held her hip, and that mouth just kept on doing everything it had done before, and more. Much more. She laughed, tried to move, couldn't. He moved lower, bringing her hands down with him and turning her onto her side, but still keeping her wrists anchored to the bed with his easy strength. His mouth moved lower, too, and she gasped.

He looked up and grinned at her. "Ready to beg?"

"Yes. Keep going."

"That's not what I meant. You're supposed to beg for me to let you go, let you move."

"I don't want you to let me go. And I'm moving all I want." It came out ragged and panting, barely in control. "I like this." She'd never said anything like this before, so simply and frankly, and it felt wonderful to acknowledge her needs and desires this way, so she said it again. "I *love* this. I love your mouth there. I love…wanting this, knowing you're going to take me over the edge."

"Oh, you do?"

"I do. Don't stop."

He didn't, not for hours. Or maybe it was weeks. Finally, she opened her arms to him and they slid together, fullness and heat, hardness and sweet, wet warmth.

Afterward, she didn't want to let him go, and so he stayed inside her and on top of her until, after minutes, he finally told her, "Can't believe you can actually breathe, Lib. I'm lying all over you."

"Breathing isn't all it's cracked up to be. How about you? I'm lying all over you."

"Oh, I'm breathing. But let me lie back and hold you now."

"Mm."

They slid apart. He stretched his arm across and she nestled her head in the crook of it, and they both fell asleep.

Scarlett woke at two in the morning, crying as if she'd had a bad dream. Libby went to her at once, without waking Brady. She found his T-shirt on the floor and put it on, aware at once of the scent of him

that enveloped her. The sleeves of the shirt reached
halfway down her arms, and the hem circled at her
thighs.

Libby didn't want to pick Scarlett up in case she
cried more in the arms of someone who wasn't
Daddy, and became harder to settle. Instead, she
leaned into the crib and stroked the little girl's back,
making soothing sounds in her throat.

Maybe Scarlett smelled the comforting aroma of
Brady, the way Libby had, infused into his shirt. The
bad dream seemed to fade, and sleep captured her
again. Libby stood there for a moment, holding her
breath in case Scarlett cried again, but, no, she
seemed fine.

But where am I going to sleep now?

After the best lovemaking she'd ever experienced,
it should be an easy choice. The hardwood floor of
the hallway felt chilly underfoot, and Brady's T-shirt
covered her inadequately. His body and his bed
would be warm beneath the thick comforter, while
Libby's own bed would be flat, unslept in and cold.
She'd given away so much tonight, and felt vulnerable. It was like vertigo, and she yearned for a safe
retreat. If she went to Brady's bed and discovered
that he didn't want her…. Scary. Giving love and
getting rejection was so scary. In some ways, it had
been easier with Glenn, because their lovemaking
had never had a lot of power for her. Her body had
never tricked her into betraying the needs she'd admitted to in Brady's bed tonight.

When she reached the doorway of Brady's room
and heard his rhythmic breathing, she continued
along the hall.

* * *

Brady awoke at around four and realized that he was alone in the bed. It wasn't the best time of night for a discovery like this.

For the first few months after Stacey's death, Scarlett would waken at around this time every night, wanting to be fed. With his energy at its lowest ebb, he would stumble down to the kitchen to warm her bottle, stumble back upstairs and carry a now-screaming Scarlett into the bed with him while she drained the bottle.

She was usually asleep again before she finished it, so then he'd carry her back to her own bed, where she'd sleep through until he had to awaken her at six-thirty to start their day. In that two-hour interval, he would count himself lucky if he got back to sleep at all.

It would probably be the same tonight. This was always when his thoughts and his emotions took on their darkest aspect, torturing him with questions and regrets.

In his marriage, those questions and regrets had revolved around the emotional balance between himself and Stacy. Should he have been tougher on her about her persistent dishonesty? Should he have divorced her, way early on, when she admitted that she'd lied about her pregnancy to get him to the altar?

Tonight, Stacy seemed a long way in his past, and he thought about Libby instead. Why had she left his bed? He wanted her here, wanted to hold her, remind her with his touch about the perfection of what they'd just shared.

But at some point while he slept, she'd gone.

The Family & Adventure Collection...

We'd like to introduce you to the
Family & Adventure collection, a wonderful
combination of Silhouette Special Edition® and
Silhouette Intimate Moments® books.
Your 2 FREE books will include 1 book from
each series in the collection:

**SILHOUETTE
SPECIAL EDITION®:**
*Stories that capture
the intensity of life,
love and family.*

**SILHOUETTE
INTIMATE
MOMENTS®:**
*Roller-Coaster
reads that deliver
fast-paced
romantic
adventures.*

Your 2 FREE BOOKS have a combined cover price
of $9.50 in the U.S. and $11.50 in Canada, but
they're yours FREE!

Your FREE Gifts include:

- 1 Silhouette Special Edition® book!
- 1 Silhouette Intimate Moments® book!
- An exciting mystery gift!

Scratch off the silver area to see what the Silhouette Reader Service™ Program has for you.

Silhouette®
Where love comes alive®

YES! I have scratched off the silver area above. Please send me the **2 FREE** books and gift for which I qualify. I understand I am under no obligation to purchase any books, as explained on the back and on the opposite page.

329 SDL DU33   229 SDL DU4K

FIRST NAME	LAST NAME

ADDRESS

APT.#	CITY

STATE/PROV.	ZIP/POSTAL CODE

Offer limited to one per household. Subscribers may not receive free books from a series in which they are currently enrolled. All orders subject to approval. Books received may vary. Credit or debit balances in a customer's account(s) may be offset by any other outstanding balance owed by or to the customer.

▼ DETACH AND MAIL CARD TODAY! ▼

©2001 HARLEQUIN ENTERPRISES LTD. ® and TM are trademarks owned by Harlequin Books S.A. used under license.

(S-SI-07/03)

THE SILHOUETTE READER SERVICE™ PROGRAM—Here's how it works:

Accepting your 2 free books and gift places you under no obligation to buy anything. You may keep the books and gift and return the shipping statement marked "cancel." If you do not cancel, about a month later we'll send you 6 additional books from the Family & Adventure collection–3 Silhouette Special Edition books and 3 Silhouette Intimate Moments books, and bill you just $23.94 in the U.S., or $28.44 in Canada, plus 25¢ shipping and handling per book. That's a total saving of 15% or more off the cover price! You may cancel at any time, but if you choose to continue, every month we'll send you 6 more books from the Family & Adventure collection, which you may either purchase at the discount price or return to us and cancel your subscription.

*Terms and prices subject to change without notice. Sales tax applicable in N.Y. Canadian residents will be charged applicable provincial taxes and GST.

DETACH AND MAIL CARD TODAY!

BUSINESS REPLY MAIL

FIRST-CLASS MAIL   PERMIT NO. 717-003   BUFFALO, NY

POSTAGE WILL BE PAID BY ADDRESSEE

SILHOUETTE READER SERVICE
3010 WALDEN AVE
PO BOX 1867
BUFFALO NY 14240-9952

NO POSTAGE
NECESSARY
IF MAILED
IN THE
UNITED STATES

Tonight, it probably didn't mean "I wish we hadn't done this." It probably just meant "I don't want Colleen to wake up in the night and find I'm not there." But he missed Libby, all the same. He wished she hadn't gone, or that she'd at least half woken him with a kiss before she left.

As he'd anticipated, Scarlett awoke in the morning before he'd managed to get back to sleep.

"Do you remember we talked a week ago about traveling back?"

Libby was stirring oatmeal on the stove for the girls' breakfast. Brady stood by the coffeemaker that sat on the bench-top, pouring black liquid into two mugs. He added milk, then handed Libby hers. He let his fingers touch her hand, and she suspected it was deliberate. His close lean and his low voice and his steady gaze were all deliberate, too. He was reminding her about how they'd felt.

"Traveling back from a kiss?" she asked.

"Yes, or from—"

"The other. Yes, I remember."

"Is that what you've done, Libby?" His voice was even lower.

"No. You mean because I moved back into my bed?"

"Yes. I woke up at four, and you weren't there."

"I wasn't traveling back. Sideways, maybe. I— You know...the girls...if they—"

"Of course, yeah. Next time, just give me a good-bye kiss."

"Next time, I will."

There would be a next time. They both knew that. They promised it to each other all through a perfect

day spent together with the girls. They didn't promise with words but with the way they looked and
touched. And maybe the day was perfect *because*
they kept promising it to each other. That night,
Libby didn't move from Brady's bed until almost
dawn.

Chapter Eight

Libby called the Toyland Children's Center first thing Monday morning and told the manager that she would take the job.

She hadn't told Brady about it, and she remembered what he'd said ten days ago about silence being a form of lying. She didn't want to believe he was right. Silence was a protection. Was it wrong to try to protect herself? Against dependency on someone else? And against having decisions bulldozed out of her hands?

She'd started to understand, by this time, how ingrained was Brady's sense of right and wrong, but he couldn't know how it was for her, he couldn't need silence as a protection the way she did. So she kept her decision about the job to herself, and made the call as soon as he'd left the house.

"How soon can you start?" Martha Dinmont asked at once.

"Well, when you need me, I guess. As you know, I've just moved here from St. Paul and I have no other commitments to wind up."

Other than going to her doctor's appointment this afternoon and—larger issue—finding a place to live. The edge of urgency had increased inside her since Friday night, and she was remorseful about the way she'd spent so much of the weekend with Brady, instead of continuing her search for an apartment.

As she'd said to him, sleeping together muddied her emotions rather than making them clearer. Or to use another metaphor she'd thought about, the needle of her compass still pointed in the same direction, but it quivered now, when before it had been steady.

If the new level of their relationship was a mistake, they'd both have to deal with the fallout, putting the needs of their girls first. If their physical response to each other burnt out quickly, it would be even more crucial for Libby and Colleen to have their own place. Would it burn out quickly? Her experience was too limited to give her an answer.

"Frankly, that's now," said the center manager, in response to Libby's statement. "We have a girl out sick today, as well as no one currently in the position you'll be filling. I realize it's a lot to ask, but…" She let her voice trail off hopefully.

"You'd like me to start today? If you can, uh, give me an hour or so to get myself together."

"Sure. Of course. You're doing me a favor. I have a part-timer who really wants to leave by lunch-time."

"And I have a doctor's appointment at three-thirty this afternoon."

"Your hours will end at three," Mrs. Dinmont promised. "I've looked at our staffing and I'll want you to work six until three."

"Okay. We talked about this as a possibility, didn't we?"

"Yes, that's right."

Libby hadn't been sure. The manager had mentioned two options on Friday, the alternate one being nine until six. Both timetables had their advantages, and their down sides.

"You're welcome to leave Colleen here while you go to your appointment. Obviously at no charge, since she's going to be a regular."

Martha Dinmont was definitely eager for her to start today. Not quite ready for this, Libby adjusted her thinking.

She and Colleen were just about ready to head out when the phone rang. It was a call for Brady, apparently a client, who told her, "I'm sorry to trouble you at home, Mrs. Buchanan, I'll try him on his cell phone again later."

She didn't waste his time or hers explaining that she wasn't Mrs. Buchanan.

The phone rang again as soon as she put it down. It wasn't Brady, as she'd thought it might be, if he and his client were playing phone tag. It was the Realtor she'd spoken with last week about the garden apartment complex across the river that she'd liked.

"You wanted me to let you know if a two-bedroom became available?"

"Yes, I did."

"We have one opening up on December one, if you're still interested."

"Can I see it? It's not the one you showed me through, is it?"

"No, it's in the adjacent block, second floor, overlooking the lawns, not the street. Let me see if I can reach the current tenant, and I'll get back to you."

"I won't be at this number."

Libby gave the number of the day-care center, then she and Colleen managed to get out of the house.

The house was quiet. Libby and Colleen weren't home.

Brady had detoured here on the way between two jobs, intending to grab a quick lunch, and on finding the place empty, he didn't try to kid himself. He was disappointed. The kitchen was immaculate, apart from a pile of sheets and towels on the floor, waiting to go down to the washing machine in the basement. The mail had arrived, and Libby had left a neat stack of letters on the hall table, where he'd be sure to see them.

She'd also put a glass spaghetti jar there, full of sprays of greenery and one lonely, late-blooming white flower she'd managed to scrounge out of some corner of the garden. Brady appreciated the arrangement more for what it said about Libby than for how it looked—although it did look kind of nice.

He'd rather have been looking at Libby herself, however. He needed the distraction.

Gretchen and Nate had taken turns sticking emotional splinters under his fingernails for half the morning. He knew they were indispensable, and he knew how long it would take him to get their replacements hired and orientated and on top of the work.

So he'd wanted to see Libby. He'd ached to see her, and ached for the way her body could make him forget that the rest of the world even existed. He'd ignored any possible suggestion of parallels between the risks Gretchen and Nate had run by getting involved when they had to go on seeing each other professionally, and the risks he and Libby were running by getting involved when they had to go on seeing each other because of their daughters.

Ducking into the powder room that filled the space under the stairs, he made a discovery.

Little soaps.

Libby had cleaned the powder room and hung an embroidered hand towel that definitely wasn't his, as well as an orange on a ribbon, stuck thickly with cloves, to keep the air freshened. In a glass dish next to the basin, she'd arranged some little shell-shaped soaps.

Hiya, fellas! I remember you from Minnesota.

This time three days ago, he might have groaned at the sight of them. Today he laughed, and knew that the little soaps weren't so much of a burden to bear after all. When Libby brought them into his life, they came with certain compensations. As he left the house, he was smiling.

Colleen clung to Libby's leg and cried when Libby tried to leave her at Toyland while she went for her doctor's appointment.

She wasn't yet twenty months old. She didn't understand Libby's promise that Mommy would always come back.

"You really want to come with Mommy?" Libby said to her daughter. "Okay, then, let's go."

Colleen stopped crying as soon as she realized that Mommy wasn't going to leave her here after all, and that they were going in the car *together*. Libby found the hospital easily enough, and parked in its multi-level garage.

She was called in to see the nurse almost at once, but had to give her medical history, which took time, and then had to wait in a cubicle until the doctor himself came in, by which time it was already five after four. At least she'd been able to keep Colleen entertained with a couple of stories.

"Okay, let's talk about what's going on in your body," Dr. Peel said, before he'd even closed the door.

Libby was out again in five minutes, with the promise of "tests." She had to make an appointment at a radiology clinic for an X ray and a pelvic sonogram.

"Non-invasive," the doctor had said, looking at her with the light from the windows reflecting off his square-framed glasses. He had pale blue eyes, pale skin and a pale, token smile. "Nothing to be nervous about."

Libby hadn't warmed to Dr. Peel, and regretted that she'd put off seeing Anne Crichton about her heavy, painful periods, before she left St. Paul. Dr. Crichton was warm and energetic and in her late thirties, with two young children of her own, and Libby had been seeing her about routine concerns for several years. Dr. Crichton was the one who'd told her that, with the discovery of Glenn's illness, they'd lost their chance to have a child.

But it was foolish to regret not making the appointment, when she thought about it. She wouldn't have had time to have these follow-up tests done in St. Paul, let alone to undergo any treatment that might prove necessary.

Dr. Peel thought that the problem was "probably just fibroids. But there are other possibilities we need to rule out." He'd ducked out of the cubicle again and left Libby to conjecture about those. He was clearly in a hurry to get through his final appointments of the day.

Based on his somber intonation, she thought immediately about cancer and felt a dread that seemed to suck her whole stomach inside out.

Cancer.

The word drummed and echoed inside her head. *Cancer.* She knew about cancer. She'd been on that roller-coaster ride already, with Glenn. Cancer wasn't always fatal, true, but it was never a quick-fix problem. If she had to undergo lengthy treatment, what would happen to Colleen? And if the treatment failed, as it had failed for Glenn...

She felt ill with fear.

As if understanding that something was wrong, Colleen stretched up her little hands and Libby gathered her against her heart, kissing her forehead and her hair. She kept her voice steady. "Let's go out to the desk, sweetheart, and make those other appointments, and then we'll go home."

No, she remembered, not home. They had to see the apartment. She couldn't let it slide.

It was the last thing she felt like doing, and she was late in getting there, but she went through with her inspection and told the Realtor after five minutes that she'd take the place. It was in good condition, it was away from the street, it faced south to admit the winter light and it was ten minutes closer to Toyland Children's Center than Brady's place was.

In the back of her mind, all she kept thinking was, "Probably fibroids? I'm a single mother with a young child. *Probably* isn't good enough."

The lights were on in the kitchen and living room when Brady turned into his driveway at just after six, which meant that Libby was home.

"Isn't that nice?" he said to Scarlett, in the back seat. "We're going to see Libby and Colleen."

And Libby was probably cooking!

"Ibby," Scarlett said.

"Yes, Libby. And your sister. Colleen."

"Toween!"

"That's right, beautiful." His heart rose like a helium balloon. Scarlett had said the name so happily, as if she'd recognized that Colleen was a great new addition to her life.

The two of them held hands going up the steps, and when Scarlett toddled inside, there was Colleen in the kitchen, playing on the floor with pots and pans, and Scarlett said it again. "Toween!"

Libby turned away from the stove where she had some sliced mushrooms frying in a pan, and water beginning to steam in a big cooking pot. She looked flushed, tired and distracted, her hair was all over the place, as untidy as spun sugar, and Brady could still glimpse the fading scratch on her arm from ten days ago. Now, however, she started to smile. "Was that—"

"Yes." He grinned. "She's saying Colleen. Said it in the car, too."

"Oh! Oh, wow!" She blinked and sniffed and stretched her shoulder across her face so that she could wipe her eyes on the short sleeve of her top, and Brady realized that she was crying. Or trying not to. She was laughing at the same time, shakily. "This is so *stupid!* What a thing to get so emotional about! I'm just a mess."

"She said Libby, too. Well, Ibby, anyhow."

"Oh, she did? Ibby, huh? That's the best thing that's happened all day!"

"Maybe I should call you that." He dropped his voice. "Give me a hug, Ibby."

She went into his arms, with a wooden spoon still in her hand.

"I'm sorry," she said, before he'd even gotten a chance to kiss her. Now her mouth was moving too fast, and she was holding him stiffly, with her arm held out behind his back so he wouldn't get mushroom juice on his shirt. "Dinner isn't going to be much. Spaghetti, with sauce from a jar I found in your pantry. I'm adding some mushrooms to ours. Colleen and I only got home maybe ten minutes ago."

"Hey. Who says you had to cook at all?"

"Well, I know you like it."

"I like to see you looking fresh and relaxed, too, instead of exhausted. You're under no obligation, Libby. What were you doing today? I stopped home for lunch, and you weren't here."

"I, uh…"

Silence.

A long enough, thick enough silence for him to

feel the stirrings of unease, and even anger. Libby
had turned back to the stove to mess with those
mushrooms. What was she doing? Buying time to
put together her story?

She was. Something like that, anyhow. Something
less than upfront. Only she wasn't as adept at thinking up ways to fob him off as Stacey had always
been.

The helium-balloon feeling in his heart deflated,
and he had the same trapped, angry, frustrated tension all through him that had sometimes seemed like
the keynote to his whole marriage.

Maybe Libby was right. So Scarlett had said
"Toween" and "Ibby"? Big deal. As she'd said, it
was no reason to get emotional. It was no reason to
want to hug Libby and feel her warm, curvy body
against his, becoming more familiar to his senses
every time they touched.

These other, too-familiar feelings, on the other
hand, grew more of a big deal with every second in
which she didn't answer him.

Finally, she took in a deep breath. "I... Well, I
started a new job today." She was still facing the
stove, and she sounded very reluctant. "It's good.
Full-time hours, Monday to Friday, with Colleen
welcome there. But there are a couple of difficult
kids, and kids with major food allergies, and it'll
probably have me feeling a little tired until I adjust.
The hours are from six until three."

Now it was Brady's turn to fall silent. He wanted
to say, "You didn't tell me," but that line sounded
too familiar, and he'd heard her probable answer before, too.

"I'm telling you now," she'd say.

They'd had this whole conversation ten days ago, in this very same room, when he'd seen that scratch on her arm. She wasn't obliged to share every little detail of her life with him, of course. And when she did give him information, he'd had no reason as yet to think that she was lying. Silence was lying. He'd told her that, but it wasn't always true. So this probably wasn't a big deal.

All the same, he didn't like it. A new job wasn't a little detail. It was a major decision, and it affected both of them. He had a right to know in advance, didn't he? He'd believed she was considering the position he'd found out about for her at Scarlett's day-care center, but she obviously hadn't been considering it at all. Why hadn't she been upfront about that?

It gave him a sense of discomfort, made him wonder if the foundation of trust they were trying to build together was still a lot thinner than he'd been imagining, especially since Saturday night.

Okay, was he going to let this go? He'd gotten very good at that, during his marriage. Just getting his head down, going on with his life, convincing himself it didn't matter. In the short term, it was the easy option, but the long term was a different story.

"So," he said at last, his voice a little tight. "Not at Scarlett's day-care center, I'm guessing."

"No. I—I really needed full-time, Brady."

"You could have been clearer on that. A heck of a lot clearer. I wouldn't have wasted your time and mine, not to mention the manager's time at Scarlett's day care, exploring the other option."

"I know. I'll…try to be clearer, next time."

What next time? he wondered at once. Did she

anticipate more situations like this? Did she already have a couple in the pipeline? More things she wasn't talking about?

"Okay, let me tell you about it now," she went on. She lifted her chin and took a breath. "It's at a place called Toyland Children's Center, out toward Dublin."

"That's a drive. Although I guess you won't be traveling it at peak traffic hours. Six in the morning is an early start."

"It is," she answered. "But that's okay. The other...uh...yes, the other thing that happened today is that I've found an apartment. Well, the Realtor called me back and offered one. You remember, the garden apartment complex that I liked? It has a two-bedroom available from the beginning of December. That will take ten minutes each way off the drive."

"That's good. So it's all worked out?"

"I wouldn't say *all*." She smiled, still looking tight and strained. "I mean, it's fine. I'm just tired."

No. There was something else going on. He'd put money on it, and he wasn't a betting man.

"Yeah, I'm tired, too, Libby," he answered her, and didn't try to hide his anger anymore. "I'm not real happy with the way you handled this."

He glanced at the meal she was cooking, irritated by her attention to this sort of detail, when they both had more important things to focus on. What was she doing? Trying to create some sixties sitcom illusion that they had a perfect little domestic life cooking away, here? Clearly, they didn't.

"And I should tell you," he added. "Make a note

of it, if you want, for future reference in the kitchen. I don't like mushrooms.''

''Right,'' she answered thinly. ''I'll remember that.''

''Can you see anything?'' Libby asked the sonogram technician.

The woman's face was focused and serious, with scarcely a muscle moving, and certainly none of the seven muscles needed to create the human smile. She moved the probe, or whatever it was called, back and forth across the slippery gel coating Libby's abdomen.

''You'll need to hear the report from your doctor,'' she answered, not taking her eyes from the screen. ''I'm not qualified to give you any kind of diagnosis.''

''Right. I understand.''

Libby lay back patiently, still hearing Colleen's earlier crying in her ears. Colleen was at Toyland, and although Libby had made her appointment for today, Friday, with the deliberate goal of giving her daughter several days to settle in, Colleen still hadn't wanted to be left. Libby sometimes wondered about how clingy she often was.

Was there, somewhere in her subconscious, a sense of abandonment after the dislocation of being left at the orphanage, and then spirited off by her new mommy to a completely different life half a world away?

No, she was probably being oversensitive to the issue. Since her appointment with Dr. Peel on Monday, Libby couldn't help viewing everything in the blackest light.

A lot of young children went through a clingy stage, she reminded herself.

Libby hadn't wanted to leave Colleen at Toyland this afternoon, but she'd been told it was inadvisable to bring a young child along to the radiologist, and now she understood why. She'd had to wait half an hour, and the test itself was taking longer than she'd anticipated, with the probe thingy being moved back and forth, and pressed quite firmly and painfully into her abdomen at times.

She had the X ray scheduled next.

As long as it's not cancer, I'll put up with any level of discomfort and pain.

Libby had been telling herself this for four days. And she'd told *only* herself.

Oh, she'd wanted to tell Brady. She'd rehearsed the words fifty times in her head. But the words sang and buzzed in her mind whenever she was with him.

On Monday night, she'd gone to him after their tense, awkward meal, when the girls were already asleep. He'd been watching TV, and she'd put a hand on his shoulder, thinking to herself, "Now. I'll say it now. And if he doesn't react the way I need, that's fine, I'll just deal with it. I'll survive."

But he hadn't given her a chance. And to be honest, she'd needed more than a chance. It wasn't fair to blame him. She'd needed a great big push. He'd thought her hand on his shoulder was the prelude to a communication of a different kind, and they'd ended up in bed just minutes later.

It was good. It was wonderful. She'd begun to understand what a considerate, generous lover he was. It was as if he could hear the music of her body through his hands. He seemed to know when his touch was right, and to know instantly and explosively when it was *so* right that seconds later she had to gulp back sounds that were almost screams.

She had a harder time being as sensitive to him. Things got in the way. Things that *shouldn't* get in the way. For example, she wasn't convinced, at first, that he'd want her to be so greedy or so honest about what she wanted. She'd never experienced a man's desire for her to be such an active partner. Monday night, when they hadn't remotely resolved certain issues out of bed, they'd definitely resolved a few in it.

He'd propped himself on his elbows above her, the shadowy dimness in the room making his face look almost fierce. She'd felt the muscles in his upper arms knotting against her ribs, rock hard as they supported his weight. She'd felt his arousal, too, between her thighs, and she'd understood what an effort he was making to hold himself back.

"Tell me what you want," he'd said. "I mean that, Lib. Or show me. Move me. Put my hands where you want them."

He'd slid sideways, freeing his hand. "If you want me to touch you here, or kiss you here, caress you with my fingers or my tongue. If you want me off the edge of the bed, kneeling on the floor. If I'm too fast or too slow or too hard or too soft, then you have to *show* it. Or say it."

And for the first time, she found that she could. In the ripe heat of her need, she gasped out simple words that she'd spoken a million times before, but never in this intimate context. "There! Yes! Oh, yes! Softer. Yes. Yes…"

Oh, she'd blushed afterward. She'd felt hot, tentative, stripped raw, and she'd waited with dread for him to deny her in some way—distance himself, close off, or say the wrong thing. But he hadn't. He hadn't said much at all. He'd just kissed her and held her in his arms. It was so nice. So good.

And of course she could have told him then about her fears. But the words had felt like balls of lead in her throat, too heavy to push out. She remembered the trauma of Glenn's diagnosis, and how angry he'd been when she'd admitted how much she was mourning the loss of a future baby.

"That?" he'd said. "I might be terminally ill, and you're crying about that? A being who doesn't even exist?"

"Who never will exist, Glenn. It's a loss, isn't it? It's a part of what we've both lost through this. It's not the only thing. I know that. But…don't ask me to separate the strands in what I'm grieving for."

"You're being incredibly selfish, Lisa-Belle."

Maybe she had been. Maybe she still was, because, lying in Brady's arms on Monday night, she'd known that she couldn't tell him about any of this. Just thinking about it made her stomach cave in.

"Okay, we're done," the technician said. "You can get dressed and wait in Reception until you're called for your X ray. We'll courier the reports over to your doctor by the end of the day."

"Can I call him for the results?"

"You have a follow-up appointment with him, right?"

"Yes. For Monday."

"He'll talk to you about it on Monday."

She remembered that it had been like this with Glenn's illness, too. There were these agonizing periods of waiting that you just had to suffer through.

She *probably* had fibroids. And Dr. Peel *probably* had no idea how endlessly long this weekend would seem to her.

By the time she got back to Toyland at a quarter after two, Colleen had cried herself to sleep.

Chapter Nine

"The two of you need to go out," Delia Buchanan decreed that same Friday afternoon.

She'd brought Scarlett home after their regular day together just a few minutes after Libby and Colleen had arrived. Brady was still at his office. "Dealing with all the garbage that gets thrown at him," Delia had said.

There was a fine November rain falling out of a sky that darkened far too early now that daylight saving time had ended, and the furnace was humming in the basement, sending warm wafts of air through the vents.

"Would you like to stay for coffee?" Libby had asked, and then to make sure that Mrs. Buchanan knew she meant it, she'd added, "Please do." She hadn't seen much of Brady's mom yet, but what she had seen, she liked.

Ten minutes later, here they were, sitting on Brady's leather couches and sipping coffee while they watched the girls playing with blocks on the big square of Persian carpet that covered the hardwood floor.

"You need some time," Delia added.

"Oh, we're doing fine," Libby answered automatically.

Probably fibroids.

The doctor will tell you on Monday.

"Well, no, honey," Delia said. "I hope you won't take this the wrong way, but you look tired and tense, and Brady's had a horrible week at work, with two of his best people quitting on him. You had the football game last weekend, but that wasn't enough. Let me get to know my new grandchild a little. Let me sit for you tonight, and you can go out to eat."

"He might prefer to go out with some friends."

"He might," Delia agreed, "and so might you. But it seems to me you need to spend a little more time together without the girls. You need to get to know each other better just as adults, not as the parent of your daughter's other half. If I know Brady, even though you're sharing the same house, he's standing back and giving you so much space you hardly know what he looks like."

Well, no, that's not exactly the problem.

Libby had a pretty detailed idea of what Brady looked like. And yet his mother was partially right. In other ways, he *was* giving her a lot of space. He'd stepped back over the past few days. He hadn't pushed in any way, and Libby found him hard to read.

Since Tuesday morning, thanks to her new schedule, the girls had stopped sleeping and waking in sync. Libby had been getting up an hour and a half earlier than Brady did, and she'd left the house before he was even awake. They'd only overlapped for an hour or two each evening, and after an evening meal and night-time routine mainly taken up with catering to the girls, he'd muttered about "work to catch up on" in his home office.

He'd still been in there when she was ready to say good-night, and she hadn't felt right about going into the room and into his arms. She'd stood in the doorway, and he'd stayed in his desk chair, and though the intervening air had heated immediately, as if someone had opened a blast-furnace door, he hadn't acted on it, and neither had she.

She didn't quite know why. It was coming more from him, she thought.

"I wouldn't mind getting out," Libby admitted to Delia.

She was due to move into her new apartment in three weeks. The two of them could discuss practical plans for bringing the girls together once she and Colleen were no longer living here. If they were going to do sleepovers, they'd need to double up on things like cribs and high chairs.

Her thought track collided with the strong sense that these issues weren't really the important ones, but she swerved away from it.

"I'll make eggs for the girls," Delia said. She added, half as a question and half as an accusation, "Brady says you cook every night."

"It's therapy."

"Even from therapy you need a night off," Delia said firmly.

"No, Tarwett! It's mine!" A little scuffle erupted on the carpet.

"They're saying each other's names?" Delia crowed with delight.

"Since Monday," Libby told her.

"And they're fighting!"

"Only occasionally."

"That has to be normal, even for twins."

"Normal is good," Libby said, as she scrambled down to floor level to resolve the situation. "Normal is *very* good!"

Brady got home to find his mom and Libby finishing cups of coffee and talking like old friends.

Libby hadn't cooked. Passing through the kitchen, he'd seen the bare, clean counters, the lack of pots and pans on the stove, and the cold, dark window of the oven. He was a real jerk to feel disappointed about it, especially since he was getting more and more convinced it was her way of wallpapering over the cracks in their relationship—an effective way, his hungry stomach said.

How could anything be really wrong, when a man came home to little shell soaps in his powder room and the smell of heaven on a plate every evening?

And that was Libby's goal, wasn't it? To make him believe that nothing was wrong. She probably would have cooked if Mom hadn't been here.

He'd felt himself brewing to a confrontation more than once since Monday night. They'd slept together after her belated revelation about the job, and his angry, inadequate reaction to what she'd said. They shouldn't have, he'd since decided. Making the moves so that they'd end up sleeping together was *his* way of wallpapering over the cracks.

Tempting and easy, but wrong. He remembered too many times when he'd let Stacey seduce him into forgetting that he was angry with her. It was okay while it was happening, but afterward the anger simmered inside him and got worse.

Sex—even *great* sex, like he and Libby had—didn't always make for a great relationship.

So he'd deliberately held back, biding his time, waiting for answers, waiting until he felt more certain that things were really okay, and they hadn't slept together since.

"You're earlier than we were expecting," his mother said.

"I threw it in for today," he answered. "I might have to go in on the weekend. The temp is hopeless. And we'll be lucky to get the Powell job back up to schedule before winter."

"Don't think about it. I'm baby-sitting tonight, and the two of you are going out."

His face dropped. He couldn't help it, and he knew both women had seen. Yeah, this was what he needed to cap his week—sitting across a candlelit table from Libby and wanting her with every cell in his body, when he'd decided there were things they had to deal with before he'd let it happen again.

Mom was glaring at him. Libby was fiddling with her clear-polished nails.

The girls, bless them, were oblivious. Scarlett had her arms wrapped around his leg, trying to pull him down to the floor to help her with her block tower. He went willingly, glad to have a way to hide his face.

It was too late, though. Mom, as usual, wasn't going to let it go.

"If you two aren't getting along," she said bluntly, "that's all the more reason to go. You *have* to get along, if you're serious about putting the girls' needs first."

"We're getting along, Mom," he growled.

Yeah, in bed. And while he wolfed down Libby's impeccable meals.

"You should still go. You need adult time. Take in a movie, too. There's time. I'm making scrambled eggs for me and the girls, and the way Colleen is drooping, I'm going to start making them now, or she'll fall asleep in the dish."

"I have to get her up at five, now, and then she naps early," Libby said, her tone an uneasy apology. "At least she'll be too sleepy to get upset when I go."

"And she'll be in her own bed," mom said. "Go get ready, Libby, and you can tuck her in bed before you leave. Brady, do you want to convince the girls it's time to tidy up the blocks? The eggs'll only take a couple of minutes."

"Sure." He was used to his mother in her take-charge moods.

Mom was a refreshing person. Even her attempts to be subtle and devious were always totally transparent. Maybe this was why it had taken him so long to cotton on to Stacey's unrepentant tactics. He just hadn't encountered such things before.

He hadn't encountered a woman like Libby before, either. She wasn't like Stacey, he'd begun to conclude, and she definitely wasn't like Mom.

She disappeared upstairs and came down again in

fifteen minutes, looking so pretty that he felt as if a
giant's hand was squeezing his chest, and he wanted
to take her to bed with him right now, whether it was
wallpapering or not.

She'd put her hair up with a gold-and-silver clip,
and she'd made up her face for evening, with darker
lipstick that made her mouth look fuller and more
sensual, and some different shade of eye-shadow that
made her eyes seem huge and almost luminous. She
wore a lacy gold chain necklace, and a matching top
and skirt that was probably silk. It swished like silk
around her body as she moved. He couldn't have
named the color or the style, but he liked it.

The top fitted close around her waist and breasts,
while the skirt flowed around her legs and hips, sil-
very-gray in some lights and pale purplish-blue in
others. Her shoes were silver-gray, too—heeled, satiny, beaded bits of nothing that could have doubled
as Cinderella's glass slippers.

"I'll...uh...change, too," he decided aloud, feeling suddenly work-stained and stale by comparison.
"While you're putting Colleen to bed."

In his bedroom, after a sixty-second shower, the
only thing that seemed appropriate was a dark business suit, which earned his mother's complacent
comment to Libby, "Doesn't he clean up nice?"

That's right, Mom, he thought. Send me out of the
house in the company of a woman I'm sleeping with
but feel like I hardly know, blushing like a beet.

He was aware of Libby through every nerve ending as they walked beside each other to the garage,
rain laying a thin cloak of damp over their coats, and
when he opened the passenger door for her and she

slipped past him, she left eddies of intoxicating desire like perfume in her wake.

They hadn't made reservations, which on a Friday night ruled out Columbus's finest dining. Instead, they settled on an upmarket chain, and were given a quiet table near the windows.

After they'd ordered, Libby leaned forward and said, "It's probably good that your mom made us do this. We should start talking seriously about what arrangements we're going to put in place three weeks from now, when Colleen and I are living on our own."

Brady just looked at her.

"No," he said. "We're not talking about that. Anything but, Libby, okay? For tonight? Anything but." She frowned, and before she could say anything, he went on, "Mom's right. We have to get along with each other. We have to talk. We have to trust. We have to do more than just jump each other's bones at night and talk about our daughters when we've got clothes on."

He saw her eyes widen. Okay, so he'd been a little crude. He wasn't sorry. She was so nervous, or reluctant to be here, or something, that she'd started shredding her napkin and wadding the pieces into a damp little ball in her palm.

He waited for one of her sweet, false, "I'm fine" type lines, ready to pounce on it, not caring that his words would probably be clumsy and he'd be crowding her, bulldozing her. He needed to learn to say this stuff.

But she pulled the plug on his motivation when she picked up a fork, started twiddling it in her fingers and said, "One of my friends made a comment I thought was perceptive before I left St. Paul."

She kept looking at the fork, so that all he could see was her smooth forehead, her creamy eyelids and painted lashes. But her voice was low, without that sweet, higher-pitched, "I'm fine" quality that set his teeth on edge. If she meant this, if it was important, then okay, he'd listen.

"She said this would be like going through the divorce without ever having the marriage. And, you know, I've been thinking about it. There's a weird logic to it. I don't like the fact very much. But there is."

"Well, I've never been divorced." Brady thought about it for a moment. "But, yeah, I can see a couple of parallels."

"You're right." She looked up, lasering his gut with those beautiful eyes. "We shouldn't talk about the girls tonight. Tell me… Let's see… Tell me why you went into construction, and why you enjoy it."

They talked for more than an hour. Half teasing, half serious, Libby proposed a penalty system under which if either of them mentioned the girls, they had to put a dollar on the table each time.

Brady laughed at the suggestion and said, "Let's see if we can *not* put in enough to leave for the tip."

They succeeded by a good margin, although there was a small pile of crumpled bills sitting between them by the time they finished the meal. By then, too, they were holding hands.

"If we're going to make it to this movie…" Brady said.

"Yes, we should go." Movies were good, Libby

thought. You could sit in the back and hold on to each other. You could even kiss. And the story unfolding on the screen took you far away from your own concerns.

Brady's body looked fine and upright and strong inside the formality of his suit. His mom had been right. He did clean up nice. Better than nice. His fingers were like cool liquid on her skin. She'd been fiddling with the silverware half the evening, until finally he'd captured her restless hand and taken the fork out of her fingers. He hadn't said anything. He'd just looked at her.

It was such a complicated look from a man who didn't usually come across that way—a mix of wariness and reproach, giving and desire, that churned up her stomach at once. She hadn't finished her soup or her salad. He must have noticed, but he hadn't said anything, the way Glenn would have. He didn't suggest dessert.

Probably fibroids.

She could tell him about it. She wouldn't even have to put a dollar on the table. But her heart sank and she felt ill every time she thought about it. The kind of solitude that came from keeping problems and fears and needs to herself was easier to withstand, she'd found, than the kind of solitude that came from admitting to something and not being truly heard.

What was that old saying? "A trouble shared is a trouble halved," or however it went. It wasn't true, in her experience, and she couldn't yet trust that when it came to the really important things, Brady would be different. He'd laid his cards down pretty forcefully over the issue of which of them should move. He'd been unhappy with her decision about the job.

Get over yourself, Libby. Just wait until Monday. He probably wouldn't even want to know about her exaggerated fears.

"Will we make it in time?" she said to Brady as they walked to the car.

"We're a little late leaving the restaurant, but watch me floor the pedal."

"No, thanks. I'll keep my eyes shut for that part."

"Kidding, Lib."

"I know."

"We'll probably miss the Coming Attractions, that's all."

The wet streets weren't empty, but they weren't traffic-jam-crowded, either. Brady got a clean, smooth run and had uncanny luck with the traffic lights until they were nearly at the cinema. Then, out of nowhere, as they crossed a wide-open intersection, a pickup truck came screaming through from the right, against a red light.

For one stark, endless moment it loomed in front of them, a wall of dark-blue metal, and Libby pressed back against the seat, pushed her feet into the floor, curled her toes, held her breath, prayed and waited for the sickening impact, the explosion of pain and the black oblivion that would follow.

Meanwhile, Brady wrenched the wheel to the left, moving violently in his seat, and rammed the brake pedal toward the floor. The red speed needle plummeted to zero, but with the misting rain that was still falling, the road was slippery and they began to skid.

The pickup roared through, missing their front bumper by inches, and Brady's car careened across the intersection on a diagonal and came to rest in front of several oncoming vehicles, which had just slowed to a stop as the light in their direction turned red.

"I'm going to get sick," Libby gasped.

"Get out of the car. Put your head between your legs. Breathe," Brady ordered. He opened his own door, pivoted his legs and planted his feet on the wet road, heaving in lungfuls of air.

Libby made it to the median strip, dimly aware that a couple of drivers had pulled over to help, while the rest were steering around Brady's sharply angled vehicle and continuing on their way. She didn't see Brady's approach, just found him crouching beside her, suddenly, with his arm wrapping around her coat-padded shoulders.

"Going to lose it?"

"No." She tried to stand up and he helped her, then they stood there looking at each other, as rain settled on their hair, while behind them the cars flowed in a curve around his vehicle. "I'm okay, now. I'm fine."

"How do you expect me to believe you when you say things like that?" His voice was harsh. "You'd say, 'I'm okay, I'm fine,' if you had arterial bleeding, Lib! Sweet jiminy!"

"No, I wouldn't," she answered, and burst into shaky sobs. "All right. I'm not okay. I'm completely not okay. I thought we were going to die, and I'm still thinking, if something happens to one of us, or both of us, if one of us—dies—what kind of position will the girls be in?"

"Put a dollar on the table."

"Brady—"

"No, don't say it. I know. I know. That's what I'm thinking about, too. We're making a mess of this. We're doing it wrong. We need to get married, so the girls are protected. Their relationship and their future. We're sleeping together. We're living together. Don't move out. Marry me, instead. Will you, Lib? Could you?''

"Brady?''

"I'm not talking about love or happy ever after. Maybe we won't be able to make it work. But—kind of a twist on what your friend in St. Paul told you— even if there's a divorce down the track, it'll protect the girls' relationship a lot better if we've had a marriage first.''

She answered him in one incoherent phrase, and then he kissed her.

They didn't tell Brady's mom about their decision that night. It was too new, and there were too many plans still to work out. After the near-accident and its emotional aftermath, neither of them was in the mood for a movie, so they arrived home early.

Delia met them at the door, disappointed. "You were supposed to stay out longer than this!''

"We're a little shaken up,'' Brady said. "Guy in a pickup almost plowed into us, at around fifty miles an hour.''

"Oh, my lord!''

"We're okay, but it felt too close for comfort.'' He put his arm around Libby, and she saw at once that the gesture hadn't gone unnoticed.

She waited for one of Delia's typically blunt comments, but she said nothing about it, asking instead, "Do you want me to stay?''

"No, it's okay," Brady answered. "Did you have any trouble with either of them?"

"They were angels. Colleen didn't stir, and Scarlett went out like a light after I read to her. I'll see you soon, then." She paused. "Look after each other tonight, won't you?"

"Maybe a little better than she thinks," Brady said, as soon as Delia had gone. "You're precious to me, Libby. You're important. I've been wanting to do this all week, but it hasn't felt right. There's been too much we…weren't talking about, or something. But now I can't let you go."

He began to kiss her, pressing his lips to her hair and her temples, her closed eyes and her expectant mouth. He touched her, confident of her response, sure of what he was doing to her body, and he was right.

"I feel fragile, Brady," she said. "That pickup was too close. And there are so many other things that could happen." She took a shaky breath. "Cancer…"

"Cancer?" His hands froze against the undersides of her breasts. "Dear Lord, do we need to talk about something like that? Tonight was enough of a scare, but it didn't happen. And cancer's not going to happen, either. Hell, Lib!"

"It did happen. To Glenn."

"It's not going to happen to you. Don't we have enough to think about without borrowing that sort of trouble?"

Libby couldn't find an answer. She let Brady cradle her again, and felt her thoughts fold in to their private, protected place in her heart where it was lonely but self-sufficient, and safe.

Oh, heck, you know, people said the wrong thing all the time. Human beings weren't gifted with that degree of sensitivity. What would she have expected, even from an angel sent to protect her?

Tell me about your cancer fears, Libby, and a few words from me will make them all go away. It's not like I'm aching to go to bed with you, or anything.

In the real world, it didn't happen that way.

They'd both been scared tonight, and they'd agreed to a marriage. It was a solution to what Libby feared most right now—that the lack of a formal arrangement between them would separate the girls forever, from each other and from their new parents, if something happened to her, or to Brady. This was the important part. They'd found a solution. That was good. It was great. She'd do better—she'd be safer— if she kept the rest to herself.

"Coming to bed?" Brady said. "I want to carry you upstairs. I want you in my arms tonight. *All* night."

He painted kisses on her neck, her ear, the upper slopes of her breasts, and she let her body sink and sigh against him. This was a kind of safety, too, the uncompromising power of their sensual response to each other. No room for ambivalence here. No room for self-sufficiency, or for holding back. She wanted him as much as he wanted her, and it made her dizzy.

"You're really planning to carry me?" she whispered.

"Future wife? I think I should. And I'm sure I can."

He scooped his hands beneath her and bundled her up, one arm around her shoulders and the other beneath her thighs. Her head bumped his shoulder, and he grinned at her and kissed her quickly. "Comfortable?"

"Ready to see if you can make it all the way upstairs."

"I'm confident."

He bounced her half into the air, and she shrieked and laughed. They'd both gone a little crazy with reaction, Brady thought, and he was giddy with anticipation and desire, as well. He loved the ripe, rounded feel of her breast pressing against his hand as he carried her up the stairs, and couldn't help pushing his hand higher, so that her breast pressed more.

Her top had dragged down a little at the front, showing a dark shadow where he would soon bury his face. He'd hold these fabulous shapes in his hands, he'd suckle her, and he knew exactly how she would sound when she cried out.

Holding off since Monday had tightened his needs, and he almost threw her onto the bed. She laughed again. Didn't mind about it. She was impatient, too. Brady dragged on his tie, pulled his shirt over his head with most of the buttons still fastened, flung his undershirt into the corner of the room then found that Libby was halfway through unfastening her bra.

She was still lying on the bed, twisting a little, arching her back and lifting her hips so she could reach around to the clasp at the back. She finished up on her elbow, with her bared breasts spilling onto the other arm, their nipples hard and dark pink.

Her body was so honest, and so responsive, meaning that he didn't feel any hesitation about the power of his own reaction. He knew she liked it. She reached around again to unfasten her skirt at the

back, and he shimmied it down for her. He planted
a kiss on her hip then let his mouth travel inward,
and she gasped and her body whipped.

"Oh, Brady…"

She scrambled to her feet and dragged on his
pants, grabbed two handfuls of his rear end through
the cloth as if too impatient to wait, and then dragged
again. At the same time, she kissed him hotly and
pressed herself against him, breasts and groin, clearly
knowing exactly the reaction she wanted, and exactly
the reaction she was going to get.

He took her breasts, suckled them the way he'd
promised himself he would, and instead of falling
back onto the bed, he lifted her and they crashed
against the wall. She wrapped her legs around him,
arched her back to press her peaked nipples against
his chest again, and they both lost it, just lost it.

He tasted tears on her cheeks and knew he was
almost sobbing himself.

At midnight, lying in Libby's arms after they'd
both been still and silent for a while, Brady said to
her, "Tell me about Glenn." His hand explored the
curve of her hip, then came to rest there, soft and
heavy. She was in no hurry for it to move.

"What about him?" she asked.

"Well, you know, anything. The important things.
The basic stuff."

"He was a regional finance manager for a national
restaurant chain. He liked golf and fishing."

"No, Libby." He eased away from her a little, and
slid his hand down to her thigh. "I put it badly. I
meant your marriage, I guess."

"That's different. That's not Glenn. It's something else. An entity of its own."

"Okay, then, your marriage. Were you happy? Was he—you know, does this exist? People say it, but I'm not so sure—the love of your life?"

Libby was almost grateful for his clumsy phrases. He didn't always express himself easily and well in words. It gave her a convenient license to answer his question obliquely.

"I was in raptures on our wedding day," she said. "Nine years later, I nursed him through a terminal illness. I was holding his hand when he died. There was love. *Care,*" she said, revising her original word choice. "No one doubts the existence of care, do they? You must have cared for Stacey. You struggled through all those years of infertility together. You were confident enough to adopt a child."

"Or desperate enough," he said bluntly. "You know, I don't—my parents didn't bring me up to—like—fall off the horse at the first piece of rough riding. I stayed the distance. Stacey had her moments. We were managing. I thought."

"But you don't think so now?"

"She was with another man when she died."

"Oh, Brady, I'm so sorry!"

"Yeah. It's the kind of thing I'm hoping I never have a reason to tell Scarlett. Never look for a reason to tell anyone things like that. Only now I'm telling you."

And it was hard for him. Even to find the words. Libby felt the effort he was making, communicated through his body, still wrapped around hers. She ached for him, listened to him with her whole heart as he tried to say a little more. And yet there re-

mained a detached space inside her, and she was in
the middle of that space, thinking, "Don't. Don't put
us through this. It isn't necessary. It's safer when you
keep it to yourself."

She hadn't betrayed nearly as much to him about
Glenn, about the destructive patterns in their marriage, and she didn't intend to.

Because you haven't escaped those patterns, yet.

Was that the reason? Why had she let those patterns build so strongly in the first place?

"Thank you for telling me," she said, as if he'd
given her a gift that wasn't quite what she wanted,
a gift that fell into the category of "It's the thought
that counts."

Then she kissed him with a deliberate, teasing heat
that made quite sure this conversation wouldn't go
any further.

"I'm letting you do this," Brady muttered against
her mouth. "Probably shouldn't." He said something
else, that she didn't catch because it was lost between
their lips. Sounded like "wallpapering." Couldn't
have been that.

"As we thought, you have some significant fibroids in your uterus, and I'd recommend surgery,"
Dr. Peel said. "Both to deal with the discomfort and
heaviness of your periods, and in the event that you
might want children."

"But it's not cancer?"

"I never talked about cancer, Mrs. McGraw."

"No, but—" Sudden tears came, like rain clattering onto a roof. "Oh, thank God," she said. "Thank
God it's not!"

The specialist surveyed her coolly, with a degree

of surprise. "I'm sure you're relieved. I didn't realize that you'd been so concerned in the first place."

"My husband—my *first* husband—died of testicular cancer four and a half years ago. He was only thirty-eight."

"I'm sorry for your loss."

"Yes, it was hard." Since Dr. Peel's statement had been formulaic, Libby's answer was, too.

"Will you go ahead with surgery?" he asked. "Or do you need more time to think? Do you want to talk it over with your husband?"

She'd mentioned a first husband, so it was logical for him to assume there was now a second. It wasn't accurate, though. Not yet. It would be in a few weeks.

"I'm not—" she began, intending to correct him, but then decided it was irrelevant. "Well, I'll go ahead, of course," she said instead. "Unless there are reasons against it which you haven't given me yet."

"There are the usual extremely rare risks associated with any surgery," Dr. Peel said. "But this isn't a major operation. At your age—" he glanced down at her file "—I'd imagine those risks would be outweighed in your mind by the positive effect on your fertility."

He waited for her response, so she said, "Mm."

"I should tell you, there are no guarantees that you'll be able to conceive easily after the surgery, but it will certainly improve your odds to a considerable degree." He looked at her file again. "There are no notes here about any previous research into your fertility. Have you ever attempted to conceive?"

"Just for a few months, several years ago. We weren't trying long enough to suspect a problem when it didn't happen. Would the fibroids have been present then? Would they have been a factor?"

"That's impossible to say, I'm sorry. Were you having symptoms?"

"Not until a few months ago. They came on gradually. It's hard for me to pinpoint the timing."

"Mm. If you do decide to go ahead, you can schedule the procedure with my staff today, or over the phone."

Dr. Peel gave one of his carefully rationed smiles and prepared to leave the room. Libby let him go, since she couldn't think of anything more she wanted to say. His manner didn't encourage casual conversation.

Still in a daze of relief at his diagnosis, she went out to the spacious waiting area and told one of the women behind the desk, "I need to schedule a procedure."

She saw her file already resting near the computer. With the appointment clerk's help, she picked a date in December, a week and a half after the wedding date she and Brady had decided on, and a week before Christmas.

Next, she went to the mall and bought a bridal gown.

Libby looked different, Brady realized as soon as she came in through the kitchen door.

Could be her pink cheeks. It was cold outside.

Or it could be the enormous white bag she carried, emblazoned with the name of a bridal store, in silver script, and the grin that appeared on her face when she saw him looking at it. Colleen's hand gripped the top of the bag with a toddler's possessiveness and determination, as if she knew it was important, too.

Brady transferred the sizzling-hot supermarket pizzas from the oven to the top of the stove. "You got it?"

She'd called him at work this morning to say she'd arranged to work a split shift at the day-care center today, starting at six and finishing at seven, so she could take a few hours off in the middle of the day to shop for a dress and handle a couple of other errands.

They both felt impatient to push their plans for the wedding forward as quickly as possible. To Brady, the prospect of a legally sanctioned and clear-cut arrangement between them was like the scaffolding he erected on his construction sites. It offered strength and safety, at a point when the final structure—a building, or in this case, their relationship—wasn't far enough advanced to do so.

It would help. It would guide them. He had to believe that.

Since Friday night, they'd already fixed a date, booked his church, found a restaurant and started calling people. "You'll get a written invitation as well," they were telling family and friends, "but with such short notice, we wanted to call first."

Through all the weekend activity, Libby had seemed so tense and distant, however, that he'd been holding his breath, waiting for her to say that she'd changed her mind.

He'd responded cautiously to her mood. His instincts had been split, as usual. On the one hand, he'd wanted to yell at her, "If it terrifies you that much, we won't do it. It was my idea, but you said yes right away. I didn't exactly have to twist your arm. You had tears in your eyes. You acted as if it was the best suggestion you'd ever heard. If you want to change your mind, tell me!''

On the other hand, he'd felt a little jumpy himself, so he hadn't pushed. He'd held back, and had come up with a couple of convenient reasons for doing so. Space was good. Men weren't the only ones who didn't like to be smothered in questions and emotions. Women could feel that way, too.

Now it seemed as if the space decision had been the right one.

She looked a lot better.

Purchasing the dress had done something for her. Crystallized something, maybe. Was that it?

Still holding the bag in one hand, she came up to him and cupped a cool palm against his face. ''Thanks for riding out my stress levels on the weekend. I'm much better now.''

''I can see that. It's okay, Lib. We've been tying ourselves in knots since the first day I called you, out of the blue, two months ago.''

''Mm.''

She looked up into his face as if there was a string of code written across his forehead that she wanted to decipher. He put his hands on her waist and drew her close. The thick paper of the bridal-store bag crackled, and the nest of silver tissue inside it hissed.

He kissed her face with soft, slow prints of warmth, and she blurted out, ''When you're touching me, I never want to talk. Talking…saying something wrong…can ruin things. Forever. And I never want to risk ruining this.''

"This" being the magic they'd discovered in each other's bodies, he understood, which existed outside of all the other areas in which they were still searching for answers.

"Good. Don't ruin anything," he answered, just happy that they were standing close, that she'd bought a dress, that dinner was hot and ready, that he was interviewing for Gretchen's replacement tomorrow, and that things were slowly working out.

"Thanks for cooking," she said.

"You mean thanks for slinging a couple of pizzas in the oven?"

"Yeah, that." She smiled. "It's hot and it's food and it smells good!"

"At what point did I kid myself that I was going to tell him about the surgery tonight?" Libby wondered much later, lying awake beside Brady in his bed, staring at the red numbers on the clock radio alarm. "Am I kidding myself now, when I tell myself it's okay if I don't tell him at all? It's not cancer. It's a routine operation. Female stuff. It's not a betrayal if I decide to deal with it on my own."

She would put the surgery off until January, when her friends were due to end their tenancy of her house in St. Paul, and she'd fly up there and deal with the house. Put it on the market? Or strip it of the rest of its furnishings and rent it out, long-term, through a Realtor? She hadn't made the decision yet.

She would have the surgery done at the same time, but she'd have to ask Mom if she'd be able to come to Chicago to look after Colleen. She knew Mom would respond better to a concrete request for help than to a more abstract, emotional plea from Libby that she get to know her adoptive granddaughter. In that sense, the surgery might have a side-benefit.

In every other way, Libby told herself, it just wasn't a big issue.

Except, if it was such a little thing, why did she have this powerful instinct urging her to keep it to herself?

Silence is a form of lying.

She'd already glossed over a couple of facts today. Yes, the choosing of the bridal gown had taken a lot longer than the doctor's appointment, but the doctor's appointment was the original reason she'd arranged for the split shift.

She could easily have said, "And I had a medical appointment, as well. Turns out I have to have some surgery."

What was she afraid of?

Think, Libby. Work it out.

She thought it had to be because of what the doctor had said about the fibroid removal improving her odds of conceiving. She and Brady were both coming to this expedient marriage with complex and very different histories in that area. She didn't want to open up a can of worms.

The marriage they were planning had such an unusual foundation. It wasn't about love, it was for the girls. She'd tried marrying for the sake of something she'd labelled "love," and after the stifling nature of most of those years with Glenn, she'd found a real form of care for him in the end. But it had been such hard work.

She wasn't looking for love anymore. Not that kind, for sure, and she wasn't convinced that any other kind was real. Brady seemed doubtful about it, too. She had a bleak dread that telling him about the surgery might blow their whole relationship into a million pieces.

As usual, she was swerving in a panic to avoid talking about flammable emotions, the way Brady had swerved to avoid the speeding pickup on Friday night. She could see herself doing it, but couldn't find a way to change. She was too afraid.

"There has to be some key to unlock all this," she thought, "but I don't know what it is, and I don't know how to find out."

Chapter Ten

Columbus had a December snowstorm the day before Libby and Brady's wedding. It left the streets, sidewalks, yards and rooftops wedding cake-white and Christmas-card pretty.

Libby's mother came from Chicago for the event.

After her negative reaction to the move back in September, Libby had been reluctant to tell her about the wedding. She'd had that familiar, sinking feeling in the pit of her stomach as she led up to the subject with small talk, over the phone, but Val had faked her out again.

Even without having met Brady, she was immediately thrilled.

She had arrived the afternoon before the wedding, just as the weather had cleared, and she was ready to help. Val had been simultaneously impressed by Brady and anxious to get rid of him, being very firm on the tradition that he shouldn't see his bride on their wedding day until the ceremony was about to start.

This surely meant, didn't it, Mom suggested, that it would be much more practical if he and Scarlett had dinner and spent the night at his mother's, while she snatched some time alone with her daughter?

Mom hadn't seemed very interested in Scarlett, and was cautious about Colleen as well.

"You know I think she's beautiful," she'd said, almost apologetically, when she and Libby had greeted each other at the airport. "I knew that from the photos. I love her, I really do. Would you give Grandma a hug, honey? No? Not yet? See, it'll take both of us a while to get used to each other. I'm just not the kind of person who takes children to heart right away, Lisa-Belle."

Mom was this way about a lot of things. Slow to adjust.

By the time Colleen was all dressed up for the wedding, Val had warmed to her. "She is *adorable* in that dress!"

So close to Christmas, Brady and Libby had chosen dark Christmas-green and -red as their colors, and for once they were dressing the girls alike. Scarlett would be wearing the exact same dress of dark green velvet with swirling underskirts and white lace trim. There were to be no bridesmaids or groomsmen, just the two little girls walking ahead of Libby down the aisle of the church, each carrying a mini bouquet of red roses.

The eleven o'clock ceremony would be followed by a restaurant lunch. Val was flying back late that same afternoon, "to give you some privacy." They hadn't planned a honeymoon, however, and were staying at home.

"Time to go, honey," Mom told Libby, hugging her. "The car's waiting outside. Oh, and your hands are like ice!"

"That's part of the job description, isn't it?" Libby joked nervously. "Bride must have icy and/or clammy hands well in advance of ceremony."

"You weren't this nervous when you married Glenn."

"I wasn't mature enough for nerves back then."

Mom didn't seem to understand how this could be true, but Libby knew that it was.

The church wasn't full. Brady had two families of aunts and uncles and cousins who'd driven up from Cincinnati, his mother, a handful of old college friends and several valued clients and work associates. His ex-office manager, Gretchen, was here; but Nate had declined his invitation. There would be no romantic reconciliation between the two of them today.

Libby's side of the aisle was even more sparsely populated. There were her mom's younger brother and his wife and their two college-age kids from Chicago, as well as Libby's godmother, who was in frail health and shouldn't really have made the trip, although Libby was touched that she had, and two friends from St. Paul with their husbands and young children.

Brady's mom was waiting in the church entrance with Scarlett. Colleen's twin was almost hysterical with excitement about an event she didn't remotely understand, and Colleen caught the mood from her with the virulence of a serious case of chicken pox.

Brady himself, Libby knew, must be standing at the altar.

Her nerves were like steel-guitar strings, stretched to snapping point, but she managed smiles for Delia and the girls.

"They're not going to go in the right direction, and they're *not* going to be quiet!" Delia warned, with a twinkle in her eye.

"We'll handle it," Libby said, her teeth chattering. They looked so cute and gorgeous. Her twin daughters. It would be a legal reality, soon, as she and Brady had begun the process of formally adopting each other's daughters.

Libby's mom peeled off Colleen's coat. Val hadn't let Libby wear anything over her dress, in case it got creased, and the bride was freezing. The church was warm, however. Libby nudged the girls ahead of her gently, and whispered, "Can you walk down to the front now, guys?"

Almost before the words were out of her mouth, Scarlett caught sight of Brady, all the way down that red carpet runner, past all those unfamiliar people. "Daddy, Daddy, Daddy," she said, and toddled off like a rocket, arms stretched in front of her and bouquet held upside down.

Colleen was not going to be eclipsed by her sister's bold move. "Daddy, Daddy, Daddy, *Daddy!*" she yelled. She dropped her bouquet on the carpet, and then she ran.

Everyone laughed, Delia picked up the bouquet, the girls reached the altar steps neck-and-neck, and all Libby could see through her sudden tears was a blur of color and light.

Brady would know exactly why she was crying.

Colleen had never said the word *Daddy* before. As
soon as Libby reached him, he took out the starched
and folded handkerchief from the breast pocket of
his dark suit and gave it to her, and she carefully
dabbed her eyes, thinking of smudged makeup and
photos that would probably get kept forever, whether
she looked like a raccoon or not.

"Good timing, huh?" Brady murmured. "With
the 'Daddy' thing?"

"Perfect!"

The two grandmothers whisked the two little girls
onto their laps in the front row, and the ceremony
began, with all Libby's fears forgotten.

Brady had never been in any doubt that Libby
would look beautiful as a bride.

She wore a pure-white gown that flowed to her
feet in soft folds. As a concession to the winter
weather, it had long, fitted sleeves, but it left no one
in any doubt about the body beneath. The neckline
was wide and curvy, showing off Libby's fine, beautiful skin, and the fabric hugged her breasts and waist
closely.

Her hair was piled on top of her head, its complicated curls and folds catching the light, and her
makeup had her face glowing with subtle, pretty
color. White beaded slippers darted from beneath the
hem of her gown with every step.

What Brady hadn't expected, and it almost
knocked the ground from under his feet, was the
strength of his own reaction. He felt as if someone
had assigned a priceless art treasure to his care, and
he had no idea of what he had to do to keep it safe
and free from danger.

He was dizzy with awe, totally daunted and dangerously exultant at the same time. They both knew what marriage was about. They had a combined total of nearly twenty years experience in the field. Was he remotely sane to be attempting it again, when he'd told himself, just a few months ago, that he never would? And was she? How sane was she? And what were her expectations?

Sometimes he was convinced that for both of them this was simply the most promising out of a poor set of alternatives, but when he watched Libby coming, tear-blinded, down the aisle toward him, in the wake of two little green velvet mischief-makers, he knew it had the potential to be a lot more than that.

If they kept the mistakes to a minimum.

If they found the right reasons for trust.

If the prospect of divorce remained a civilized potential escape route, rather than a pressurized chemical mix, primed to explode.

During the crucial part of the ceremony, his head was cooler than he'd expected it to be, and he had time to think, Yes. *Till death us do part.* That's still accurate, even if this marriage doesn't last. We'll stay in touch because of the girls. Friends, I hope, and with respect for each other.

When he kissed her, it meant what it was supposed to mean—not a preview of their physical response to each other, put on like a show for the congregation, but a sealing of the solemn promises they'd just made.

''I'm wondering if it would be possible for you to get any time off work in January, Mom,'' Libby said as she drove her mother to the airport for her flight late in the afternoon.

She'd changed into black stretch pants and a big pastel sweater, and had left Colleen at home with Brady. Both girls were deep in the oblivion of a late and desperately needed nap, after the excitement of the ceremony and reception lunch had kept them awake and buzzing for hours longer than usual.

"Well, I probably could," her mother answered with her usual caution. "Depending on the reason."

"I need to have some surgery. I have some uterine fibroids that need to come out, and I'd like my gynecologist in St. Paul to do it, when I come up to deal with the house."

"You'll be selling it now, of course."

"I—uh—I guess it doesn't make sense to keep it. But I haven't decided yet." She felt a twist of ambivalent regret as she turned into the short-stay parking lot and began to look for a space near the terminal building. The house had been such a strong symbol of independence and self-sufficiency for her over the past few years.

"It definitely doesn't make sense to keep it," Val said. "You don't need that extra work and worry. You've got no ties in St. Paul, now. And Brady's place is lovely." Her voice got foggy. "I'm so glad this has happened, Libby!"

"Yes, it gives the girls more security, legally."

"Well, not that. It's more— You can see now that I was right to be concerned about the idea of your adopting a child on your own." Her mom's speech gathered speed and force. "It's so much better this way, Libby! Brady is obviously steady and successful and reliable—the kind of man you can depend on, like Glenn was, and you *need* that. A woman needs that, especially when she's a mother, no matter how much she might pride herself on coping alone. I'm so glad you were lucky enough to find it a second time.''

Libby turned into a vacant space and jerked the car to a halt. ''That's not why I married Brady, Mom,'' she said, feeling her anger and impatience rise. ''It was why I married Glenn, yes, and it was— it was—'' Lord, she'd never actually said this before. She'd glossed it over, even to herself. ''Too naive of me. A terrible mistake.''

Her mother gasped. ''You can't say your marriage to Glenn was a mistake! He was a good man. He cared for you. He provided for you.''

''And he took his price for it.''

''What do you mean?''

Why did I start this?

Val looked wide-eyed, worried, disbelieving, the way she'd looked all through Libby's nine years of marriage whenever Libby had let slip the slightest suggestion that anything was wrong.

How could she explain? It was all so intangible.

Val would have understood the betrayal of physical cruelty or verbal abuse, and would have supported Libby in freeing herself from such things, but Glenn's quiet, self-centered domination had been so much more insidious, disguised as the ''taking care of you'' that Mom valued so much.

Libby had interpreted it that way, too, for far too long. By the time she had matured enough to understand what was really happening, she had found herself locked inside patterns she couldn't break.

It was stifling, soul-destroying, and she hadn't realized the fact until his illness had changed the balance between them. Then he'd clung to her until his death, reviving feelings in her heart that had been in danger of vanishing altogether. She'd grieved for him, but maybe, she now wondered, she'd forgiven him too much.

Mom wouldn't want to know about any of this. Not when it was all in the past, and not when it went so much against what Val had always wanted to think. She'd recognized her mother's fragility in certain areas since she was a child, and had always protected it.

"Nothing," Libby said to her. "It's not important now."

"No! You're right! It isn't! You see, Libby? You're being unfair. You were always unfair to Glenn. Don't make the same mistakes with Brady."

"I hope I won't."

More than Val knew!

"Can we talk about something else?" Libby asked, after a moment. "What do you think about January? I need to schedule the surgery, and this seems like the best plan. If you could stay for several days and look after Colleen while I get the house taken care of, as well. There's a limit to what I can do from this distance. The surgery isn't a big deal, but I'll still need some time to recover before I can travel."

"What about Brady? Can't he take time off?"

"I—I don't want to ask for something like that so soon."

"See? This independence of yours, Libby, it just makes trouble for someone else. Of course I don't mind doing it. I'm your mother. But I think you're underestimating Brady. You're underestimating your marriage.''

"The girls aren't awake yet?" Libby asked Brady when she got home from the airport and found a quiet house.

It was already 6:30, and he was sitting on the couch watching TV, still in his wedding clothes.

"No, I think they're planning on sleeping through.''

Still in *some* of his wedding clothes, Libby revised mentally. He had his suit jacket off, his shirtsleeves rolled, his tie loosened several inches and the top two buttons of his shirt undone.

"They need it!" she agreed.

He had his bare feet propped on the arm of the couch, and when she took her eyes off him long enough to look at the coffee table, she discovered there was a picnic on it. Smoked salmon and caviar, crackers and cheese, French bread, French cakes and a bottle of champagne.

"So, looks like we might get a bit of a honeymoon, after all," he said. He looked at her, his gray-blue eyes sexy and smoky and wicked, and she couldn't focus on the picnic anymore. Her nipples tightened and her insides felt like hot, melting fudge. "Should I open the champagne?" he added. "Oh, wait! Oh, shoot! I forgot! We had the girls still running wild when we got home and I— *Shoot!*"

"What?"

"—never carried you over the threshold."

"Oh. Oh, right." To both of them, it suddenly seemed like a huge omission. Aloud, Libby tried to talk herself out of it being a big deal. "I guess it's, you know, not as if this was a new place for us. Or a regular marriage," she said.

They looked at each other again. Then he said, "Damn it!" and rolled to his feet. "Get your jacket back on!" She'd slipped it off just a moment ago, and dropped it over the back of an armchair. He picked it up and held it behind her.

"We're really going to do this, Brady?"

"Damn straight!"

"You've got no shoes on."

"I'll handle it. Some people walk over hot coals. It's okay. Now, it's gotta be the front door."

"Start at the bottom of the steps." She'd caught his mood, now.

"And I'm going to prop the door open with the stopper so it doesn't blow shut in our faces."

"Good plan."

They were laughing when they went down the steps, and still laughing when he brought her back inside in his arms, eyes fixed on her face. She waited for him to say something solemn and romantic, but he didn't.

And that was probably a good thing, given the practical foundation for their marriage. Instead, he tipped her gently onto the couch and reached for the champagne. "We're going to make this work, Lib," he said.

Christmas preparations overtook them the day after the wedding. The holiday was only a little over two weeks away, and neither of them had done anything about it yet.

The pace of the construction industry eased off over winter, but Libby's hours would be just as long.

Toyland Children's Center only closed on Christmas Day, and, a week later, for New Year.

Libby apologized to Brady about it—about having to squeeze Christmas preparations into the weekends, about being too tired, most evenings, to talk about gifts. They had to co-ordinate their purchases so that both girls would get roughly the same things. There were only a few shopping days left by the time they'd drafted a list of what they intended to buy.

But the obvious solution didn't seem to occur to Libby.

She could look around for a less demanding job.

Or she could give up work altogether.

Brady didn't mind the idea of supporting her for a few years until she was ready to go back to kindergarten teaching, if only because it would mean he'd be able to take Scarlett out of all those hours of day care.

It was wrong the way they were handling this, now that their marriage was a reality. They still weren't operating as a family, and he didn't know how to make it happen. It wasn't just his problem, however. It was Libby's, as well. He knew she was working too hard, trying too hard, thinking too much.

He couldn't find a way to confront her about it, however. Aware of how hard he found it to put emotions successfully into words, he hung back, reluctant to push, or create a crisis.

Outwardly, everything was fine. When the two of them had such good times together with the girls, and with each other, Brady didn't see how he could turn around and rock the boat by saying, "I want you to give up your job."

If Libby was unhappy with the situation, wouldn't

she do something about it? And there was more to all this than just the job, wasn't there? He could state his feelings forcefully on that issue, and still end up with huge problems.

The tension began to wind tighter inside him, and he got to that same point he'd been at before the night they agreed to marry, when he felt ambivalent about sharing a bed with her because he didn't know what it meant. Their marriage wasn't about love, and it wasn't *just* about sex. So what was left?

Most nights, Libby went to bed early after her pre-dawn start, and he was relieved—okay, physically tortured, sure, but emotionally relieved—to find her already asleep by the time he arrived.

The days passed. They shopped and stayed up late two nights in a row to get the gifts wrapped because Libby got jittery about leaving it until the last minute. They decided on what dishes they were going to contribute to the big midday festive meal at Delia's with the Cincinnati cousins. And then, three days before Christmas, they gave the girls an early evening meal and went shopping at the garden center for a tree.

"It's too mild for doing this, isn't it?" Libby said as they drove. Even so, she was hunkered down inside her heavy Minnesota coat.

"There speaks a girl from the north country," Brady teased her. "It's in the thirties."

She kept looking round at the girls in the back seat, as if wanting to check if they were enjoying this yet. Since they couldn't remember last year's Christmas, and only had a hazy idea of why they'd been taken out after dark, they actually weren't. They were just sitting there quietly.

"There should be snow piled everywhere," Libby

insisted. ''And it should be cold enough to snap your fingers off. Around seven degrees.''

''You can have seven degrees and snow. I'll take the thirties, with bare ground.''

She laughed. He liked that. He could almost always make her laugh.

But then, as he parked the car right beside one of the open gates into the garden center, he found himself wondering if this wasn't another of the illusions that only seemed to be deepening in their relationship. More wallpaper.

Yeah, sure, they could whack a few funny lines back and forth, like Ping-Pong balls. They could enjoy each other's company. But Libby held back so much that his trust about what lay beneath was getting thinner, not deeper. And that was wrong.

Since the girls were already running ahead into the forest of cut and bundled trees, Brady let it go for now, the way he'd let it go so many times before and turned his attention to more immediate matters.

Choosing a tree was one part science, one part art, and one part pure serendipity, Brady always felt. You could never really tell how it was going to look until you got it home and unwrapped, set on its stand and decorated.

Given this reality, he didn't believe in taking forever, nor in examining every tree in the lot. He liked to look at a reasonable, representative sampling of two or three different species, then make a decision. He suspected, too, that the girls wouldn't stay excited about this for long. Christmas was still just a word to them, wrongly pronounced as ''Tissmiss,'' and the Santa at the mall on the weekend had made both of them cry in fright.

"This one's nice," he said to Libby, after they'd spent twenty minutes looking at the indoor displays of Santa scenes, nativities, snow and animals, that were set up for the children, and had come outside again.

"Okay," she answered vaguely, hugging herself in her coat. At least she had it unzipped, and the hood pulled back. Her hair was a spun-sugar mess that made him want to bring handfuls of it to his face and inhale its sweet, nutty scent.

"Well, I mean, what do you think? Do you like it?" he asked.

"Yes, it's good. The right height." Seeming oddly uninvolved, she turned away from him and said quickly to Scarlett, "Honey, let's not touch the wreaths. Stay with—with me. With Mommy." She still seemed to have trouble using that word when she wasn't talking to Colleen, although he didn't doubt how much she loved Colleen's twin. "Isn't this beautiful? Look at all the lights?"

"Or there's this," Brady persisted. "It's too thick around the base, but I can cut it down. It's a good shape."

"Yes, it is," Libby agreed.

"Maybe too tall?"

"Actually, I think so. You're right."

"Or we could cut off the top. There'd still be room for an angel, or a star."

"Sure."

"How about over here? The Douglas firs? Do you have a preference?"

"Uh…" She had a get-me-out-of-here look on her face, and Brady didn't understand it. He wasn't pressuring her, was he?

Selecting a tree together was supposed to be fun. As far as he could tell, she'd seemed okay with it until they'd actually got out here amongst them all. She'd been focused on the girls, on the pretty displays indoors, and on telling him it should be colder.

He stopped twirling the Douglas firs around on their stumps of trunk and came up to her. She almost flinched, and looked around at the trees. "There's lots," she said, in a strange tone. "There's heaps. Go for it, Brady."

All the big issues of trust and communication and sharing that they were mired in, and this was the thing that had made him crack, that made him confront her as he'd known he had to do. Just this. Picking a tree.

"Okay, Libby, what is it?" he said, putting his hands heavily on her shoulders. "This time, I'm going to ask you about it, and you're going to answer me. This time, we're not getting distracted, I'm not telling myself it doesn't matter, that I need to give you space, and we're going to *talk!*"

His voice was quiet and controlled, but Libby had no doubt that he meant business, and that she'd be crazy to pretend there wasn't a problem. Even so, the answer that came out was inadequate, and she knew it. "I guess I'd just forgotten that I don't really enjoy this very much."

The memories came flooding back as she spoke, with an intensity that almost winded her.

Icy-cold Minnesota air, aching-cold Minnesota snow. It wasn't pretty, magical, Christmassy cold when she stood there in it for so long as the token, acquiescent partner. It was dead cold, empty cold, cold that mirrored all the dead, empty places in her marriage. And she had to ignore the cold, in the tree lot and in her marriage, because it seemed she was the only one who felt it.

There were so many trees, and all of them were pretty much the same. Somehow, though, the choice assumed an enormous importance. There was a range of minor variables. One tree might have a couple of thinly greened branches, another might have a crooked trunk. Sometimes it had felt to her as if Glenn was determined to examine every single one.

"What do you think?" he'd say.

Time and again, she'd answer, "Yes, that one's nice," and he'd reject it and keep looking. Occasionally, just occasionally, she'd say, "That one's a bit fat," or "That one's flat on one side," and he'd move on and then it would always seem as if the fat tree or the flat tree was the one he'd come back to.

"No, after all," he'd say, "I think I like this one. This is the one we'll take," and she was never sure, really, that he didn't do it on purpose.

Maybe he honestly hadn't noticed that he'd picked one of the trees she'd told him she didn't like. Except that, actually, not noticing was almost as bad, because it meant that, as usual, her opinion, her feelings, her*self,* didn't really count.

Later, he would praise her pretty decorations approvingly and she'd think, locking herself back into her obedient box, "Well, I guess the tree isn't so flat. The flat side's against the wall."

"What, Libby, too much choice?" Brady said. "Too much green? What?"

"No," she answered, still thinking of tree-shopping in Minnesota, when she'd had no choice at all. "Too little."

"There's a thousand trees here!"

"Okay, so choose," she yelled, whipping herself out from beneath his heavy hands on her shoulders. "Just choose." Her voice cracked. "Get it over with, please, and let's go."

"We're choosing together, aren't we? Libby, talk to me." His voice was a low rumble. "*I* thought we were." He studied her face. "Choosing together."

"If that's what's really happening…" she said.

"It is, Lib. If you're not enjoying it, let's make it quick. Tell me your three favorite trees, off the top of your head, just the ones you can see from here, and I'll pick one out of those. Isn't that fair? Isn't it? Talk to me! The girls are running wild. We need to get out of here."

"Fair? You care about whether it's fair!" She started crying, but she was laughing, too. Heaven help her, she was hysterical, crazy. Feeling like this! Reacting like this! Over a tree!

"I love that. That's so simple," she sobbed. "Oh, listen to me!" She laughed, sniffed, sobbed again. "It's so obvious. Why couldn't Glenn ever have thought of that?"

"This is about *Glenn?*"

"Oh. Yeah, or about me not standing up to him, or something. Because at first—at first—when we met, I—I guess I needed it, for some reason?" She frowned. "But, oh, after a couple of years, I got so frozen, and we went back and forth, trees and trees and trees, and nothing I said mattered. And every year I'd—slow learner, sucker for the Christmas spirit—I'd *forget.* How much I hated it and how long it took and how cold I got and how defeated I felt as we drove home, because, as with everything else, there was nothing I could do to make him see there was a problem.''

''But you've bought trees since.'' He was still challenging her. ''You've had four Christmases since.''

''I got one of those little artificial ones, around three feet high, and put it on a pedestal in the window. It was white and silver, it was pretty, and it was mine. I hung it with golden balls and green lights, and it looked like something out of a magazine. This year, in the car, I was thinking about the girls, and how they'd run around and get excited.''

''Yep, they're doing that.''

''And that they'd get even *more* excited when they realized what we were going to do with the tree when we got it home, and then suddenly, with all these stands and stands of trees, and my coat, and it not being cold and snowy enough, the other part of it, all those married-without-children Christmases, they all came back.'' She shook her head. ''Like every other decision in our marriage. Glenn made it. Never consulted me, because it was his right. He earned the major money.''

''You never stood up to that?''

''I—I tried. Not hard enough. Guess I felt… At least he was *there,* thinking about the two of us, putting his energy into the relationship, even if it was done in a way I didn't like. You know, he never let me take a permanent teaching position because he wanted my working hours to be flexible so they could fit in with his. I didn't like per diem teaching. I wanted a kindergarten class of my own, so I could stay with the same kids all year and watch them learn and grow. But, you know, he never listened. He said

I was selfish. I—'' she shook her head ''—guess he convinced me it was true. I definitely felt self-*contained*, after a while.''

He held her and kissed her, looked into her face. ''Okay, I know this doesn't solve everything, but... Choose. You choose. Whichever tree you want.''

''I liked your idea better.''

''Yeah?''

''Yeah, Brady. I'm going to pick three, right now, and then I want to see which one of those you choose.''

They'd traveled an important distance tonight. Brady was convinced of it, and it gave him a giddy, happy, lightheaded feeling that he didn't quite know what to do with. From Libby's selection of three trees, he picked a big Douglas fir, and they paid for it and he wrestled it onto the roof-rack he'd clamped on top of the car.

At home, the girls thought it was great that they were going to have a big, resin-scented blue-green, real live *tree* in their living room, and they didn't want to go to bed. But it was late, and they were tired, so they eventually did, which left Brady free to trim down the base of the trunk, fix it into the stand and set it up in front of the window to settle overnight. They'd decorate it tomorrow.

While he was working on the tree, Libby heated up some pea and ham soup she'd made earlier. He lit a fire for the first time this season, and they sat in front of it, watching the flames and drinking their soup out of mugs, just like his mom did. Brady discovered it was good that way.

Libby was quiet, obviously tired. She didn't say

much, but Brady felt that even after what she'd said at the garden center, they weren't finished yet. He decided to push. He decided he had to *learn* to push, and now was a good time to start.

"Libby, what you told me tonight about you and Glenn and choosing a tree, and the other stuff—"

"I...uh...that, yes. You listened, and—"

"No, no, hang on. I'm guessing it was pretty difficult and miserable at times. I'm thinking you made changes after he died."

"Redecorated the house from top to bottom." She smiled. She was trying to keep it light, but he didn't want it light right now.

"More important changes than that," he said.

"I, yes, I enjoyed discovering more independence."

"And is that why you don't want to consider giving up that ridiculous job?"

Okay, bad move, bad wording. He'd lost her. He saw that at once. She'd retreated into politeness. Wallpapering. Any second now, she'd ask him if he wanted more soup and he'd probably yell at her. Which wouldn't help.

"I didn't realize," she said politely, "that you had problems with the job."

"I just—I don't," he answered quickly. Not truthfully. "Well, the hours. I thought you'd want—Scarlett and Colleen aren't spending much time together."

"More than we initially planned, since I haven't moved out."

His fluency returned in a fresh rush of anger. "Libby, we planned squat! We were flying by the seat of our pants. We still are. If we'd been married to each other from the beginning, and if we'd had the girls together from the beginning, we wouldn't be doing it like this.''

''Well, no.''

''Is there any *way* two parents would do it like this with siblings, let alone identical twins? We wouldn't have them at day care on opposite sides of town. Mom's asking about it. When does she get to have Colleen on Fridays, too? And if Colleen can wear little pink outfits every day, why can't Scarlett? I want you to give up the job.''

It hurt, Libby discovered.

It hurt to a stupid extent.

It probably should have made her angry, and she should have attacked back, challenged his right to issue such an abrupt command, but instead she just felt as if she'd been hit in some exposed and vulnerable spot, and reacted in her usual instinctive way.

She hid what she felt.

She took the last gulp of soup, masking her face behind the mug, then said, steady and polite, ''What are you suggesting instead?''

''That you don't work at all, for a few years. Or at most, that you work part-time. I'm jealous, Libby—jealous that Colleen has you with her all day and Scarlett doesn't. I feel like they should be together during the day, because if they're not, why have we done this? I look at how tired you get, too, getting up so early, working with other people's difficult kids all day while you're trying to have something left for Colleen—and for Scarlett—and there just doesn't seem a lot of point to it, when you don't have to.''

''Is it possible that I enjoy it?''

"No. Don't tell me that. I've seen how you look when you get home. You don't enjoy it enough to work those hours."

"I'm not going to let you bully me into this, Brady."

"I hope I don't ever bully you," he answered quietly. "I said what I wanted. I thought it would be a factor for you. I thought Scarlett's needs would be a factor for you, too."

"They are. But she—I—"

"It's okay. Keep the job if it's important. For whatever reason. We'll forget this conversation ever happened."

"I don't know how to work this out."

"Forget it, I said. It's late. I guess you want to get to bed. I'll clean up, okay?"

"Thanks."

When Libby went upstairs, she folded herself into Brady's bed, as usual, instead of into her own, mainly because she was afraid that if she didn't, if she slept alone, he'd want to challenge her on that issue, too.

Chapter Eleven

"Are you sure you don't want me Wednesday, Lisa-Belle?" Libby's mother asked on the phone. "I can change my flight."

"Thursday is fine," she answered. "The Thursday morning appointment with Dr. Crichton is just a preliminary, just routine, to make sure I'm fit for the surgery on Friday. Colleen has a play date with my friend Angie and her daughter. Angie and I will visit a little, and then I'll try and get some sorting-out done at the house during the afternoon."

"So you're selling?"

"I'm still not sure. I want to see how I feel about the house when I see it again."

"Then I'm coming Wednesday," Mom said. "You won't get anything done at the house with Colleen underfoot. In any case, honey, I'm getting so excited about actually spending some time with her."

''I'm glad about that, Mom.'' Libby recognized that her mother was trying to make amends for hanging back for so long.

The days had flown by over Christmas and New Year, and Libby's scheduled surgery was just a week away. She continued to struggle with the question of telling Brady, but had no new answers. She'd read enough pop psychology articles in magazines to know that communication was supposed to be a good thing in a relationship, but what happened if the only feelings you communicated to each other were negative? Was silence still a form of lying?

This whole thing was happening in her own body, and she didn't want to risk an input from Brady that might be wrong. Her fear about it seemed out of proportion, however. Even when they'd argued, the day they'd bought the Christmas tree, it hadn't killed them. Why did this scare her so much?

Almost as soon as she'd put down the phone after talking to her mother, Libby heard Brady and Scarlett outside. As it was Friday, Scarlett had been at Delia's today.

Knowing that Brady would have overheard a crucial part of the conversation if he'd arrived just two minutes sooner, Libby experienced the familiar stab of guilt and panic that was only growing worse as the days passed.

She wanted this marriage to work. She and Brady got on so well when they joked with each other and talked about day-to-day things. The girls had loved their Christmas, and it had been a joy to watch for both adults.

Scarlett and Colleen had found their gifts when they first woke up, in stockings hung on the mantel-

piece and beneath the tree. They'd torn the paper off
with shrieks of excitement to find tricycles, blocks,
dolls, chocolate coins covered in gold paper and
other delights.

Brady and Libby hadn't even attempted to open
their gifts to each other until the girls had finished.
Libby had bought Brady a jacket in soft brown
leather. It was a very personal gift, a wordless tribute
to how much she loved his body—its strength and
its tenderness. He had given her jewelry, and she
loved the fine white gold he'd chosen, in matching
bracelet, necklace and earrings.

Both of them admitted at the end of the day that
they'd enjoyed the time they spent with just the two
girls and each other more that the busier Buchanan
gathering later in the day.

They both had to hang on to positives like this.

Mindful of Brady's criticism of her long working
hours, Libby had begun to put even more effort into
keeping the house immaculate and the kitchen productive. As well, she'd started picking Scarlett up
from day care at the end of her own working day so
that she could spend an hour or two each day playing
with both girls before Brady came home.

Did he appreciate her efforts? Did they rob him of
his conviction that she should give up her job? She
wasn't sure. They hadn't talked about it.

"Have you arranged for any Realtors to come look
at the house?" he asked her half an hour later, as
they ate.

"There's one who's happy to handle a sale or a
rental, and she's going to take a look at it on Thursday afternoon. I'll make a decision by then."

"It's your call, Libby. I've said that."

"I know. Thanks."

"It should sell pretty fast, shouldn't it, and rent out just as easily? It's a nice place."

"I hope so."

Brady reached across the table and took her hand. "I appreciate that you were willing to uproot your life. I know it was harder for you than you said when it was happening."

"It was the sensible option," she answered. "I had less to uproot than you did."

"I didn't know you very well, then. I think I bull-dozed you into it."

"I guess I let you because there were good reasons."

"We're still allowed to fight about things, Libby. We can fight it out, when we disagree."

"Oh, you're telling me we don't fight enough?"

He laughed, then frowned. "Weird, but true. We don't. And I think that's my fault, too."

The red numbers on the clock radio showed 4:03 a.m. when Libby rolled over in Brady's bed and looked at it in the dark.

It was five days after that strange statement of his about fighting—that she couldn't agree with—and she was flying to Minnesota today. It would be a long day, and she should be sleeping, but she'd woken at three and still her mind wouldn't slow down. Brady lay beside her, a big, warm, familiar shape under the hump of thick quilt, and even the fact that she was awake and he was asleep seemed to emphasize the distance between them.

It'll be better once I've had the surgery and dealt with the house. I'll look for a better job. This is working in the ways we wanted. Scarlett calls me Mommy now. The girls are really starting to act like sisters. Sometimes it's as if they can read each other's thoughts.

So why was she so convinced, deep in her heart, that this wasn't enough? What more did she yearn for?

For no reason that she could pinpoint, a scene from her past flashed into her head—the night Glenn had asked her to marry him.

"We love each other," he'd said, and she'd felt giddy with happiness that he took such a momentous thing for granted and was willing to say it out loud, to declare his ongoing stake in her life. "We should get married."

She hadn't thought of this memory in years, but now, as she revisited it, she heard his words from a very different perspective.

He never had *asked* her to marry him. He'd never said, "I love you," and listened for her reply. He'd made a declaration for both of them, without room in his mind for doubt.

We love each other.

And he hadn't said, "Will you?" He'd said, "We should."

Even if she'd had the sense to doubt him, she wouldn't have had the courage to tell him he was wrong. For some reason, back then, she'd needed Glenn's easy, authoritative certainties. Why? She'd been just nineteen. In college. Feeling grown up. Her father had died a year earlier, but she hadn't seen him or heard from him or had anything to do with him for six years before that.

Her breathing got shallow and tight and painful.

Why was she thinking of this now? She almost never thought about her teen years. Or about her dad.

Brady was still asleep. His breathing was heavy, soft, rhythmic and soothing. He always slept on his side or his stomach, and he didn't snore. She snuggled closer to him, needing the body contact. Their physical response to each other was the strongest strand in their relationship, she often felt. Maybe it shouldn't have been. Probably the strongest strand should be their shared commitment to the girls, but in that area, there were boundaries still in place.

My fault.

Although she rejoiced in Scarlett and Colleen's growing closeness, Libby knew that she herself still had blocks and barriers. She'd taken Scarlett into her heart, but at the same time she pushed her away, didn't try to make more time to spend with her. She was so aware of how vulnerable love made her.

If she let herself love Brady, it would be the same. Or worse.

Beneath the covers, she slid her hand onto Brady's hip. Touching him was safe. Touching him was right. She nestled even closer, nudging her knees into the bends behind his, pressing her chest against his back. He was sleeping topless, with just a pair of stretchy navy pajama pants, while the thin cotton nightdress that Libby wore shut out some of his body heat and very little of anything else.

She let her arm drop across his bare, hard abdomen.

And she wanted him.

No illusions about why. Because the times they made love were the times they were closest, and she was going away today, back to a place where she hadn't known him, back to a place she hadn't wanted to leave, and she didn't know how she was going to feel, a week from now, when she got home to Columbus again.

Libby had never before awakened Brady because she wanted to make love.

Floating out of a deep sleep like a boat floating out of harbor on an ebb tide, he took a while to realize that it was happening. At first, he was only aware of her warmth and the motionless pressure of her body against his back. When his groin began to grow heavy and full, he was still more asleep than awake.

But then her fingers began to move. Softly and slowly, she started to caress him, pouring awareness onto his stomach and chest and hip and thigh like pouring maple syrup onto a pancake stack.

Wanting more, his whole body was now wide awake, but he kept up the pretense of sleep. You couldn't be a voyeur, in your own bed, with your own wife, and with your eyes closed, but that was how he felt. Like a voyeur.

If she thought he was still asleep, then she thought she was alone.

"Brady," she said softly. "Brady…"

And there was such yearning emotion in her voice that he had to move, and hold her, and kiss her. He had to slip that semitranslucent nightdress up over her head and feel her naked body against his, breasts already peaked and swollen, back arched, skin craving his mouth, hips rocking against his arousal.

"Was this my idea?" he asked her, his voice

creaky with sleep. He knew it *wasn't* his idea, but wanted to hear what she'd say.

"Well, no, but I wanted you to think it was. Guess that part didn't work."

"You're allowed to need this, Libby."

"Wasn't sure if I was allowed to wake you up for it."

"Did I grunt and roll over?"

"No…"

"Remember that!"

Oh, she would, Libby knew. She'd remember that…and all of this…for the rest of her life.

The hot chocolate cascaded over Scarlett's front before Brady could cover the distance across the kitchen. Somehow, her curious fingers had managed to pull the lid off of her sippy cup, and she was sticky and soaked.

Crying, too. The drink had only been lukewarm, so her tears were more from shock than anything else, and his own reaction didn't help. He yelled an exclamation and lunged at her, and she thought this was something terrible.

"Hey," he said, as he unstrapped her harness. "It's okay. So you got wet? Big deal! We're going to give you a rinse over the sink and dry you off and change your outfit."

Pity about the meeting he was already running late for.

After Libby had woken him out of a dream at four in the morning—and the reality she'd given him was much better than the dream—he'd been so deeply asleep when his alarm had sounded at six-thirty that he'd hit the off button, thinking hazily,

"I'll just grab another five," and hadn't surfaced again until seven-ten.

His meeting this morning started at eight, and was taking place on one of his construction sites, half an hour's drive away. It was now seven thirty-five, and he still had to get Scarlett to day care. No time to take her upstairs and give her a proper wash.

He pulled off the chocolate-drenched blue-and-green plaid playsuit and the undershirt beneath, held Scarlett over the sink in the crook of his arm and rinsed her off, drying her with a clean towelling dish-cloth that didn't quite do the job. She was still a little damp.

There was a basket of clean, folded laundry sitting beside the door to the basement. Libby only left laundry lying about when she was running late for something, and he had the dim idea that she'd slept in this morning, too. Hadn't he heard the side door close and her car start just after he killed the alarm?

The basket of laundry helped him in his own doomed quest for punctuality. He rummaged around for an undershirt, and grabbed an outfit of Colleen's that was sitting on the top of the pile. It was the pink dress and leggings with the little white stars that she often wore. Scarlett happily held up her little arms and lifted up her feet one at a time, while he put it on.

He'd call Libby later and explain why he'd put Scarlett in one of—

No, damn it, he wouldn't!

It was crazy that they were still dressing the girls so differently—that there were still Scarlett's outfits and Colleen's outfits, Scarlett's car seat and Colleen's car-seat, Scarlett's dad and Colleen's mom, and Scarlett's life, separate from her sister's.

He and Libby had been living together since the end of October, and they'd been married for more than a month, yet Libby went on clinging to these artificial lines of separation and he couldn't think of a good reason why.

Her bad first marriage?

Okay, he thought he understood that. Not that she ever said straight out that it was a bad marriage, but he'd heard enough of the truth from her now, in the few stories she'd let slip. The Christmas tree. The kindergarten class.

So he tried to give her space. Space to dress Colleen in pink, when Scarlett wore everything but, because he wasn't on the ball enough with laundry to keep pastel outfits stain-free. Space to keep on with that insane job, having Colleen with her there even on Fridays when Mom would have loved to take care of both the girls.

But he kept waiting for Libby to shift the lines, to need less of the space, and she never did. He kept thinking he was giving her enough reasons for trust, but the trust didn't happen. He'd gotten better at confronting her, knew he was making progress of his own in getting over his own past. He understood that Libby had deeper reasons for her evasions and her silences than Stacey had had for her more flagrant lies. He was confident that he'd moved on from his marriage.

Sometimes he felt as if he was closer to loving Libby than he'd ever thought possible, and then at other times, like now, when he found himself wanting to apologize for putting Scarlett in an outfit that belonged to her identical twin, damn it, he wanted to write Libby off like a bad debt, write off their whole marriage, give up on any thought of working it through.

Libby and Colleen were flying to St. Paul this afternoon, and he felt edgy about it. He'd offered to keep Colleen here, so Libby could work more efficiently and maybe cut short the trip, but of course she'd said no. Her mother was coming to help. It would be, quote unquote, "fine."

Of course.

He'd almost said as a challenge, "Okay, so do you want to take Scarlett, too?" but he'd suddenly had a thought so terrifying it made his stomach drop like a broken elevator. What if they didn't come back? There was something about the way she was preparing for this trip that spooked him, something in her preoccupied attitude. What else was going on?

The lack of trust between them, he realized, went both ways, and he wasn't in a good mood, three minutes later, when he and Scarlett left the house.

"And, once again, I'm so sorry about getting in late this morning," Libby said to Martha Dinmont.

"We were quiet. It wasn't a problem. I hope things go smoothly for you with sorting out your house."

"Thanks."

Sorting out the house.

Having the surgery.

"I'm just going to change Colleen now," Libby went on, "And then I'll head off."

She picked up her daughter and went into the center's baby change room to remove a pair of paint stained mauve corduroy overalls and a white and mauve turtleneck, and replace them with a one-piece pink stretch cotton playsuit, with a high, gathered waist and a sprinkling of little white flowers. She wanted Colleen to look pretty for the flight, but wanted her comfortable, also.

The traffic was about what she'd expected between Toyland and Brady's, and she had some time to spare when she got home. The laundry basket still sat by the basement door, but its contents weren't as neat as she'd left them. Brady must have been hunting around for something.

She smiled. He had a difficult relationship with laundry, and it was kind of cute, sometimes.

She sat Colleen in front of a toddler music video and refolded the messed-up laundry items, then went upstairs to put everything away. From the window of her room, a few minutes later, she saw Brady's car turn into the driveway and disappear into the garage beneath where she stood.

She hadn't expected him home, and felt her heart lift to a dangerous height. She'd thought she wouldn't see him for a week. He'd been deeply asleep when she left the house this morning, and still naked beneath the covers. She'd wanted to say something to him, hug him, follow up on their recent love-making with some words about missing him, about keeping himself and Scarlett safe until she got back. Watching him sleep, however, she hadn't dared.

Now maybe she'd have the chance, after all.

"We're still here," she called to him down the stairs.

"I hoped you would be," he called back, on his way up. Scarlett must have run into the living room, hearing the sound of the video.

"Okay, I—I'm glad," Libby answered. She was breathless, which was ridiculous.

They met at the top of the stairs.

"Can't stay long," he said, his voice a low growl.

"No, neither can I."

"I'm dropping Scarlett at Mom's and going to a late meeting with a potential client. But I needed to see you."

"Did you?"

"Uh…yeah."

Brady rubbed his fingers along the roughness of his jaw, and felt his anger and his fluency desert him. Libby's eyes were shining and her mouth was soft, and she was looking at him as if she wanted him to kiss her, not yell at her.

Hell, of course she wouldn't want him to yell at her! The problem was, *he* didn't want to yell at her, either. Not anymore. The need to yell had evaporated like spilled liquid on a hot pavement. He wanted to kiss her as much as she clearly wanted to be kissed. Sweet jiminy, this wasn't going to solve anything!

And he couldn't remember, at the moment, why that mattered, or what there was to solve. He answered the silent speech of those expressive lips and came forward. "Gonna miss you, Lib," he said softly. "Colleen, too. Scarlett'll be lonely."

"I—I know." She looked up at him. "Take care of her. Be safe. It's only a week. But then I might… uh… not be feeling too great when I get back. Oh, Brady…" She went into his arms, pushed her forehead into his shoulder, then kissed his neck.

"I know," he said. "The house."

She didn't answer, just stood quite still in his arms, then turned her face up and kissed him almost desperately. Her lips parted and her whole mouth was urgent and fast and hard against his.

He kissed her back.

Of course.

When had he ever been able to resist kissing this woman?

Something wet touched the corner of his mouth and he realized it tasted salty. She'd teared up, and a couple of the tears had spilled out of her closed eyes. He tried to kiss the tears away, touching his lips to her closed lids.

"When you get back," he said, "we're going to talk about some changes."

"Yes," she answered. "We are. I want to, Brady. Doesn't make sense, how hard it always feels. But right now—"

"Yeah, I know. The flight."

"I have to go. I have to get Colleen. The cab should be here any second."

Their bags were already by the door. He watched her hurry down the stairs, then followed her at a slower pace. She disappeared into the living room, picked up a little girl and came into the front hall again, lifting the diaper-clad bottom into a better position on her hip in preparation for shouldering her carry-on bag.

Only one problem.

It was the wrong child.

Libby was in a hurry. She probably still had tears in her eyes, and Scarlett was dressed in Colleen's pink outfit. Colleen must have gone to the kitchen looking for Mommy, or something, and Scarlett was the only twin left on the couch.

Brady saw the exact moment when Libby realized

her mistake. She gasped and gave a little cry, let Scarlett sway back a little from her shoulder and took another look, as if wanting to make absolutely sure. She said, "Oh, sweetheart!" in a shaky voice, then hugged her and looked back up the stairs at Brady, who'd stopped half way down.

"Would it really have mattered?" he said harshly, all his earlier anger coming back in a flood.

"If I'd taken Scarlett to Minnesota, instead of Colleen?"

"Yes. Instead of. As well as. Dressed the same, or dressed differently. *Would* it have mattered?"

"How come she's dressed like this?"

"She poured hot chocolate down her front at breakfast, and I didn't have time to hunt up the right outfit. I pulled the first one off the pile in the basket, and it was her sister's. Why do we still have them dressed like they're from different planets, Lib? Why do we still have Colleen's outfits and Scarlett's outfits?"

"I didn't think you liked pink."

"And you apparently don't like red or navy or plaid. But there's room for compromise. And anyway, hell, do you really think that's the issue? It's not about their outfits, it's about *them!* How come Scarlett's still mine and Colleen's still yours? You gasped and looked up at me as if you thought I'd suspect you of kidnapping her. You moved seven hundred miles so they could be together. We're married. Aren't they *ours* now?"

She blinked back more tears. Colleen could be heard, coming through the living room and calling for Mommy.

"No," Libby said. "They're not. That's wrong. I

know it is. I thought our marriage would make a difference, but it hasn't. Or not enough. I'm too scared to let it happen. And I don't know how to change that.''

"Maybe it would help if you'd admit to yourself that, for no fault of yours, your first marriage was miserable. Lord knows, mine was! If you don't admit it, your second marriage is heading the same way. I'm not Glenn, and you're not Stacey. We'll blow this thing apart in our own unique way, but we'll do it just as effectively, the way we're headed now. Is that what you want? Will you push us to a divorce and then claim custody of my daughter as well as yours? Or will you just drop Scarlett like a hot coal and never see her again?''

"Good grief, Brady!'' She'd gone white. "No! Neither of those things.''

He felt a wash of relief that couldn't dissipate his anger. "One good point, I guess,'' he said tightly. "For the rest, think about it. You've got a week. If we can't do better than this, we're going to end up writing off the whole deal.''

She was still white, but now her eyes were flashing. "I'll never let that happen. I won't let Colleen lose Scarlett, and I won't lose her, either.'' She put Scarlett down and picked up Colleen, who'd appeared a few seconds ago and was clinging to her legs. "I hope that's an empty threat, Brady, even though, I should tell you, empty threats don't impress me. I've come that far, at least. It's not threats I'm afraid of, it's what's real.''

"Yeah, well,'' he muttered behind her, as she opened the door and went out to the cab which had just pulled into the driveway. "Right now, empty threats seem to be all I've got.''

Chapter Twelve

I had a miserable first marriage.

On the airplane, with Colleen asleep in her lap, Libby said the words in her head, testing them for truth, pushing back the qualifying phrases that automatically sprang up after them.

Until Glenn's illness.

Then the bad patterns changed.

Did they? she wondered. Or did Glenn just lose the opportunity to dominate as he got weaker? In the hospital, he hadn't been able to dictate the day-to-day details of her life, and the big-picture issues had faded in the light of the biggest issue of all—that he was dying. What about the care she thought she'd discovered for him then? Was it, after all, no more than the care she'd have felt for any human being in the grip of a terminal illness, cut down in their prime?

I've made too many excuses for both of us. He's gone now. I can't lie to myself anymore. And I need to look more closely at other things.

"I had a miserable first marriage," she murmured.

The man in the seat next to her turned in her direction with a frown.

"Practising my French," she said, putting on a smile.

Okay, so I did, she decided. It was miserable, and I didn't do the right things to try and make it better. But how does admitting to this help now?

Brady had said that it would, but she couldn't see it. He'd predicted that their own marriage was headed the same way. Toward the rocks.

Regret and pain coiled deep in her gut, and the sense of loss she felt was her own. It wasn't just for Colleen or Scarlett.

I'm the one who'll grieve for what we could have had. I'm the one who'll really lose.

She loved Brady.

The fullness of her heart came as a revelation, and wasn't welcome. Love wasn't enough. She had mistakes to undo, blocks to work through—and without fully understanding what those blocks were, she still knew she'd been trying to work through them for months and probably longer, without a huge amount of success, so what on earth made her hope she'd be able to succeed now, just because one thing in her life had changed? Just because she'd discovered that she loved Brady?

What a slippery, misty, intangible word it was, too! So she had a name for it? Did that mean it was real?

Yes. Oh, yes.

It was like putting her eye to a telescope and seeing only a blur, then twisting a lens and suddenly discovering a million stars, crystal-clear. She wanted Brady in her life forever. She wanted him throwing his daughters up to the ceiling, and making them shriek with delight. She wanted him accidentally dyeing his undershirts blue. She wanted him closing his eyes when he was lying in her arms, as if he could see heaven behind his lids because of the way they'd touched.

He told me to give up my job. Did I need to hear that?

No.

But he hadn't forced the issue. He'd just made his feelings known.

I need to get better at doing the same thing.

Scary. Impossible. Because—because—

Because when I do that, I lose. I learned that when I was twelve.

No, loving him didn't solve anything. It was only the start.

Colleen stirred in her lap, and the plane began its descent, bringing Libby back to earth and back to the rest of her life.

"Hi, Val," Brady said. Libby hadn't been gone for long. Her mother must have been hoping to catch her. "You've missed her by an hour, I'm sorry."

"Oh. Oh, all right. I just thought of a question about the surgery. Did she drive to the airport?"

"No, she took a cab. What surgery?"

"That's good, because with some procedures you're not supposed to drive for a couple of weeks. Or except...I know she's planning on renting a car

in St. Paul, so I hope it'll be okay for her to return it.''

"What surgery, Val?"

There was a blank silence at the other end of the
phone. "Well, she told you, didn't she?"

"No." His voice sounded as if it was coming from
a long way away. "If she'd told me, I wouldn't be
asking."

"Oh, I've caused a problem. She should have told
me she didn't want you to—"

"No. She should have told *me*. I'm her husband.
What's this about?"

Cancer.

She'd mentioned it once.

He'd assumed she was talking about Glenn.

And she'd let him hang on to that assumption.

"She has some fibroids in her uterus that have
been giving her trouble, and they have to come out,"
Val said.

"Fibroids," he echoed, dizzy with relief.
"They're not dangerous, are they? *Are* they?"

"No, they're just troublesome."

Troublesome. Meaning "painful," he guessed. Of
course Libby hadn't said a word. If she'd been taking
pain medication at any point, she certainly hadn't let
him see. And if she'd suffered, she'd, as usual, suffered in silence. Sweet damn, but it made him angry!

"She wanted her doctor in St. Paul to do it," Val
was saying. "Dr. Crichton. Even though it's just routine. I guess that's why she didn't tell you. Because
it's routine."

It wasn't why. Brady knew it. But he let it pass.
He wasn't going to have his mother-in-law presiding

over the death of his marriage. Or over its resurrection. He didn't yet know which it was going to be.

His whole scalp was tight with anger, and he couldn't keep the emotion out of his voice when he told her, "I'm cancelling everything here and I'm flying up. First flight I can get."

"Libby will be fine. She's strong."

"Libby is not fine. She's a mess inside, only she runs her whole life so other people won't realize the fact, and so she doesn't have to face it herself. She tries too damned hard! And I'm not letting this go. I've been dealing with it for long enough."

"Well, I guess I'll see you in St. Paul, then, Brady."

"Look, no, is it possible for you to—" He stopped and tried again. "I want to handle this on my own. I'd appreciate it if you could at least delay your trip. I'll look after Colleen and Scarlett until you get there. If our marriage has even the slightest chance—"

"My lord, your *marriage?*" Val gasped.

"That's where we're at right now. I'm sorry to have to say it so bluntly. But I spent eleven years with a woman I couldn't have an honest, productive conversation with, and I'm not going through that again. This time, if it comes to the crunch, if we can't find a way to talk this weekend, I'm going to burn my boats and get out."

It hurt him even to think of it, but he knew it would be worse if he hung on to something that was just an empty, dishonest shell.

Libby picked up a rental car at the airport and checked into the motel room she would be sharing with her mother and Colleen. It was still only just

after 4:30 in the afternoon, and her mom's flight
wasn't due in until eight this evening. She had said
she would take a cab to the motel, in case Colleen
was already asleep.

The motel felt claustrophobic, and Libby decided
she might as well go to the house, try and get something done and a decision made.

Rent out, or sell?

She could order in a pizza when Colleen got hungry, and meet Mom back at the motel later in the
evening.

The sun was dipping low in a clear, ice-cold sky
when she reached the familiar street where she'd
lived for most of her marriage and for more than four
years afterward. Beneath its white winter frosting, the
house looked dark, and inside it was cold. Her
friends, Stephanie and Richard Sawyer, had left the
place looking nice when they'd moved out on the
weekend, but they'd lowered the thermostat way
down.

Libby turned on the lights and turned up the heat.
If the two little Sawyer boys had left finger marks
on the walls or spills on the carpets, everything had
now been thoroughly cleaned.

She wandered the rooms slowly, as the temperature quickly began to rise, while Colleen ran back
and forth. "Do you remember this house, honey?"
she asked. "Yeah, you do. It's not so long ago, even
in your little life."

But Colleen was too young to feel any nostalgia
or regret.

Searching her own heart, Libby couldn't find those
emotions, either. She'd expected to be swept with far
stronger feelings about leaving this place, but any

regret she felt concerned Brady. They'd both been angry. She couldn't believe that Brady would sabotage Colleen and Scarlett's relationship, even if he gave up on their marriage. He wasn't that kind of man. Lord, he just *wasn't!*

She had to cling to this knowledge. She had to attempt to trust it, and to trust him. He would never use a child as a weapon or a pawn or a bargaining point. He would never harm an innocent soul that way. He wouldn't drop Colleen from his life, the way Libby's own father had dropped her. It was one of the reasons she'd fallen in love with Brady. He never played those kinds of games. *Any* games. He was straight as an arrow. He knew what loving a child meant. And he wasn't a coward.

"I'm going to sell the house," Libby said aloud— to Colleen, or maybe just to herself, to hear how it sounded.

And it didn't hurt to say it. It felt like a step forward.

She went down into the basement with Colleen, and there was the big plastic climbing fort and slide she'd left for Stephanie and Richard's boys. It was the one that Colleen and Scarlett had first played on together, that day four months ago when Brady and his daughter had come to the house.

A few weeks later, Libby had brought it in for the winter, and she hadn't shipped it to Ohio because she hadn't known if it would fit in an apartment, or if she'd get a place with a yard.

It would fit just fine in the yard or the basement at Brady's.

She stood for a long time in front of the climbing fort, while Colleen played peek-a-boo with her through the big round holes in the sides, and slid up and down. Finally, she peeled off a blue sticker—her code for items she wanted shipped back to Ohio—and stuck it onto the thick plastic.

It was a statement of determination and faith that almost gave her vertigo. If Brady wanted to abandon their marriage, her own determination wouldn't count, but she had to recognize that determination in herself, all the same. No matter what happened, she was staying in Ohio, at least. She couldn't do anything that would part her from Scarlett, or part the girls from each other. After an hour, she'd used up two sheets of blue stickers, and only a few red and green ones—code for items to be sold or given away.

She and Colleen had finished eating pizza in front of cartoons on TV when headlights beamed into her driveway at around seven. She at first thought this might be Richard and Stephanie, dropping in to check that she was satisfied with how she'd found the house.

But it wasn't Steph and Rich at the door. It was Brady, with Scarlett in his arms.

For about twenty seconds, the two adults just stared at each other, while arctic air flowed past them into the house. Brady had his thick, navy-blue padded coat on, with the collar pulled up around his ears. It emphasized the strength of his shoulders. His head was bare, and his breath plumed like white cotton candy.

"Come in," Libby finally said. "It's freezing out there."

"I took a chance that you'd be here," he told her, striding past.

"Well, yes, I'm—"

"And not at the hospital. Your mom called just after you left."

Her stomach gave a lurch that made her instantly queasy. "I guess she told you."

"She didn't say when the surgery is scheduled for. We didn't get that far." He put Scarlett down, while Libby shut the door behind them, and they both watched as the two girls caught sight of each other.

Colleen immediately said, "Tarlett!" and scrambled off the couch. "Mommy, Tarlett's here!"

"I know, honey. Isn't that great?"

"P'ay toys inna basement." Colleen pulled on her sister's arm and they trundled off together.

"We'd better go down with them," Libby said.

"Sure. Your mom's not coming till tomorrow, by the way." Brady's voice was heavy.

"I don't—I talked to her this morning. Is she sick?" She opened the basement door and switched on the light, and they followed the girls down.

"I told her she wasn't needed right away. That I could take care of you for a day or two." Still that same heavy, wooden tone, angry and implacable.

Her scalp prickled. "Shouldn't that have been my decision?"

"I'm your husband, Libby. You're talking about decisions, and who has the right to make them? You don't even give me basic information!"

"Because I don't want you to react like this. Barging in. Taking control. Dictating procedures and outcomes. Not giving me a choice."

"That's incredibly unfair." His voice had dropped now.

The girls were playing together on the climbing fort, and he obviously didn't want them knowing that something was wrong. He didn't want them getting used to the sounds of hostility between two adults, the way some children quickly had to. His care didn't surprise Libby, but wasn't enough to put out the fire of her anger.

"You told my mother not to come," she said in a fierce whisper. "That's not taking control?"

"You're saying I did it with no provocation? You're telling me this didn't start with you, Libby?" He was standing closer than she wanted him, leaning his hand on one of the basement's supporting metal poles. She was aware of all the things about him that sent her dizzy—his strength, the fire and unflinching steadiness in his eyes, the male smell of him like fresh-cut wood. "You must have known for weeks that you were having this surgery," he said. "Dear God, when Val first let it slip, I thought it must be cancer."

"So did I," she blurted out. "For a whole week. When I was waiting to have the scans and hear the results from Dr. Peel."

"Who the hell is Dr. Peel? Your mom said Dr. *K*-something. Keighton."

"Crichton."

"So who's Dr. Peel?" He hadn't taken his eyes from her face.

"The gynecologist I saw in Columbus. The one who diagnosed the problem. But I didn't like him, so I decided to have it done here."

"Where—conveniently—you could get away with not telling me, the way you try to get away with not telling me *anything* you don't absolutely have to, in case… What, Lib? In case what?"

"I—I don't know."

"You do. I can't believe that. You damn well *do!*"

"I've talked about Glenn. You got more out of me— You *helped* me," she corrected herself carefully, "to say more, and see more, about Glenn and about my marriage than anyone else has. You're right. My marriage was miserable."

"Yeah, good. You said it."

"And I got so sick of—oh, lord!—of not being *heard,* that I stopped talking. Can't you see why that might happen? And somehow, even when I started to understand that, it didn't help me to stop reacting that way. It didn't help me to start talking again. I tried to tell you. A couple of times. I got up my courage, then something would happen—"

"Convenient, again."

"Yes, it was convenient! Sure, you're right. I grabbed on to those convenient moments—when you'd...kiss me, or something...and the courage slipped away again."

"You couldn't be that scared of what I'd say. There aren't that many terrifying options, are there?"

"You could have said, 'Get over yourself with Dr. Peel and have the surgery in Columbus.' You could have said—"

"Would that have destroyed you?"

"Would you have said that?"

"No, not if it was important to you to see the *K* doctor."

"*C.* Crichton. Anne Crichton."

"*C. X. Q.* Hell!"

"Maybe I was just afraid of getting disappointed. I didn't want to find out that you didn't know how to listen." She spread her hands. "That doesn't sound like much. I don't *know* why this is such a problem, Brady. I know you're not Glenn. I know I'm not Stacey.''

''Yeah, this is our marriage,'' he said on a growl, ''and we'll destroy it in our own way, right?''

''Right,'' she echoed thinly. ''Except I don't want that to happen.'' She looked at him, and then at Scarlett and Colleen on the plastic slide.

''Neither do I.'' They were both silent for a moment, knowing that nothing had really been decided about the future. Brady cleared his throat and said, ''So, the surgery. Tell me about it. When is it?''

''I have an appointment for a preliminary checkup tomorrow, and if everything is okay, I have to fast from midnight and get to the hospital at seven on Friday morning. I should get discharged Saturday, and I'm scheduled to fly back Wednesday. You knew I was flying home Wednesday.''

''Yeah, but I had a different picture in my mind about what you'd be doing while you were here. Isn't Wednesday too soon to fly?''

''I've asked. Dr. Crichton said it would be okay. I'm sure I'll be fine.''

He made an impatient, disgusted sound, levered himself off the pole he'd been leaning on and paced around. ''There should be word police, and they should outlaw you from using that word.''

''What word?''

''*Fine.*'' He turned back to her. ''Do you have any idea how often you say that? It's fine. I'm fine. I'll be fine. Particularly when it isn't true. I wish you'd work out why. Okay, so I'll take you to your appointment tomorrow, and take care of the girls while you're with the doctor.''

"I was going to leave Colleen at a friend's, having a play-date."

"You can do that and hopefully she'll take Scarlett as well, but let me come with you to the doctor, Libby, please? I'm not ordering. I'm just asking. I want to be there. And I'm taking you to the hospital on Friday, too. I'll be there when you wake up, if they'll let me. I checked into your motel, by the way. Same floor. Different room. Which I think is about where we are in our marriage, right now, don't you?"

Libby couldn't disagree with that.

Chapter Thirteen

"Feeling okay?" Brady asked quietly.

Libby's friend Angie had kindly agreed to look after both girls this morning while he brought her to the hospital for the surgery. She had disappeared for a while, in care of a nurse, and he'd had to sit in the waiting room for close to half an hour, stomach tight with tension.

A different nurse had just called him in to say that he could stay with his wife, now, if he wanted, until she was wheeled into the operating theater. Yes, Brady had told the nurse decisively. He wanted.

"Getting a little drowsy," Libby said. "Which is kind of nice. I'm not nervous anymore. Dr. Crichton came and said hi. And the anesthesiologist. They asked some questions. Same questions."

"I think they do that in case you remember something you forgot before."

"Guess so."

She'd had a premed injection, and she was lying on a gurney in a blue hospital gown, with a sheet covering most of her body. She slid a hand out from beneath the sheet and Brady took it, folded it in half across her palm, chafed at it. Fiddled with it, you'd have to say. He was more nervous than she was, at this point.

They were quiet for a few minutes. There was a lot of waiting around in hospitals. Staff walked purposefully back and forth on their rubber-soled shoes or their disposable blue shoe covers, and there were clattering sounds, and voices and strange chemical odors. Shut away here in a tiny, half-curtained-off cubicle, Libby and Brady were left to themselves and no one took any notice of them.

"Can I talk?" Libby asked, sounding very groggy.

"Only if you want to."

"I want to. I was thinking last night. Couldn't sleep. I'm glad you're here, Brady."

"Yeah, I'm glad, too. Glad you're glad." He squeezed her hand harder, just feeling happy that they'd both said it, even though it was such a tiny piece of communication.

It was stupid. He knew they needed so much more than this.

"And I think I'm glad Mom's not, yet." She thought about it for a moment, with her eyes closed. He almost thought she'd gone to sleep. "Yes," she finally said. "I'm glad. I love Mom. I want her to love Colleen. That's why I was pleased when she said she'd come. She's slow to adjust."

Her voice sounded funny. It was slurry and wobbly and slow. Much better than before, in some ways.

She'd been very tense on the drive from the motel, to her friend's house, to the hospital. He'd asked her what she was afraid of, and all she'd said was, "The worst."

Yeah, he was scared of that, too.

"After my dad left..." she said, then stopped again.

"I'm listening, Lib."

This is the first time she's talked about him, Brady realized. That's interesting. That's *really* interesting.

"...Mom pretended for, oh, months, even a couple of years, even once we were in Chicago, that it was temporary," she went on. "You know, when I wanted to see if I could visit more, or if he could come visit us, she'd say to me, "Let's just wait." And it was the same when my uncle invited us on a trip. "I want to wait." All sorts of things, she kept waiting. And I didn't realize for so long—maybe I was even grown up, and it was...yes, I'm sure it was...after my father died—that she was putting all her decisions on hold, ready for when he came back."

"Was she protecting you, maybe?"

"She thought she was. More, she was protecting herself. Getting to grips with it gradually. That she was on her own. That she didn't have someone to depend on. It was hard for her."

"And for you."

"I still don't know why he reacted that way," she said. Her voice was fuzzy, and then it cracked. "I'll never know."

"What way, sweetheart?" Brady asked her, the tenderness slipping out so naturally he hardly noticed. He was a little confused. The way "he" reacted? Hadn't she been talking about her mother's reaction, not her dad's?

"I put my heart on a plate for him, and he ate it for breakfast. Dear God! I was twelve! And I was so praxical about it."

Her voice slurred, and she didn't correct the mispronounced word. Practical? Was that it? She was very sleepy, very loose-tongued.

"I really thought about it," she said. "I remember lying in bed, thinking about it, and coming up with these great answers. I *thought* they were great. Hardly able to wait till morning. Horseback riding and Disney World."

She swore.

He'd never heard her do that before.

Ever.

"Such innocent things," she said, her voice sad and bitter and bewildered. "Why did it spook him so much? Horseback riding and Disney World. I said it. And then I never saw him again."

"Libby, sweetheart—" he began.

The curtain of the cubicle screeched back on its rod.

"All set?" said the nurse. "Going on a little trip to the OR, now." There was an orderly standing behind her.

Libby had closed her eyes again. Her face was very still and pale, and she had no makeup on. Her hair was pulled back under a disposable blue cap the color of a cartoon character's hair. She looked about fifteen years old. "Uh-huh," she nodded, and tried to smile. "Take me away."

"Mr. Buchanan, you'll have to stay out in the

waiting room,'' said the nurse. ''Or there's a cafe-
teria, if you're hungry.''

''How long before I'll be able to see her?''

''Not until she's ready to go up to her room, which
will be on Level 5. It'll be a couple of hours at
least.''

''I'll check on our girls, and come back. Will they
be able to see her, too?''

''Not until regular visiting hours. Three till four
for children and non-relatives. She'll still be pretty
sleepy, even so.''

''Mm,'' Libby agreed.

Brady wanted to kiss her, but the orderly had
started to maneuver the gurney, and Libby herself
already looked as if she was miles away. He watched
her go, with odd little details of the scene standing
out for no reason. One of the gurney wheels
squeaked. The orderly had very meaty knees. The
nurse seemed to be looking for the next patient she
had to check. Brady felt as if time was going very
slowly, and as if Libby was about to disappear over
the horizon of a featureless desert, hundreds of miles
wide.

''Can you find your way back?'' the nurse asked.

''Sure, yes,'' he answered. ''Through this door?''

''That's right.'' She smiled, then stopped in her
busy tracks and looked at him for a moment, as if
she could read the lines etched on his heart. ''She'll
be fine, Mr. Buchanan.''

''Yeah,'' he answered huskily. ''That's what she
always tells me.''

Libby counted backward from a hundred the way
she was told, and got all the way to ninety-eight. A

quarter of a second later, she woke up in the Recovery suite, to find someone pestering her to tell them she was okay. Or alive. Or something.

"Yeah, eventually," she said.

"Sounds good," said the voice.

"Thank you."

"Want to open your eyes for me?"

"No."

"I like 'em when they're honest."

She was left alone for a while, and her eyelids got a little lighter. Only weighed around six pounds each, now.

I guess I've had the surgery, she thought. Distant pain—several miles distant, but undeniably real—confirmed the theory.

Was Brady here? The girls?

She got one eye open, but couldn't see anyone, and couldn't move. If her eyelids each weighed six pounds, the rest of her body weighed a ton. "Hello?" she called, voice as scratchy as an old gramophone record.

"Feeling a little better?" said a voice that still wasn't Brady's.

"Some. Am I on Level 5?"

"Not yet. This is Recovery."

"Right."

"You'll be going up soon. We just need to make sure everything's as good as it looks."

"Mm."

Sleep seemed like the best place to wait, even when the nurses were taking her blood pressure and her temperature and her pulse, so she waited in sleep for a good while longer, and awoke to find that she was traveling.

It was a lovely journey, trundling along on the gurney's slightly bumpy rubber wheels. Corridor, then swing door, then elevator, then corridor again. She didn't have to know where she was going or open her eyes or speak. She didn't have to do anything at all.

And then she heard Brady's voice. "Lib? Libby?"

She tried to describe why she couldn't answer him properly. "I'm on vacation. But I'm coming back soon." That kind of covered it.

"She's been saying some interesting things like that," she heard him say to someone.

"Sometimes they do."

"How should I—? I mean, if she says something that seems significant, should I remind her about it later?"

"Ask her if she went to Cozumel or Acapulco on her vacation?"

"Well, no. It was before she went under. When she was getting sleepy from the medication. She was talking about her dad."

Was I? Libby thought. Oh, I was. I was.

She'd been thinking about him half the night. Things she hadn't let herself think about for years.

"Disney World," she said, to show that she remembered, and that he was right. It was important.

"There you go. She went to Disney World."

"No," Brady said. "Really. It was before the surgery."

"Wait a while, then, sure, remind her. Worst can happen is that she's forgotten."

"Yeah, I'll do that. I'll have our daughters with me. Might have to wait."

"Where are the girls?" Libby said, getting both

eyes open at once, just for long enough to squeeze out a little smile at Brady. Oh, he looked…good. Just good. Right. The right person to be here. Her eyes closed again, but the picture of Brady stayed in her mind.

"Angie said they were doing fine at her place," he answered her. "Both of them happy. I wanted to see you before I went to pick them up. I can bring them in to see you at three, apparently."

"Good."

Sleep pulled on her and wouldn't let her go. Someone made her move from the gurney to a bed and she had to crawl and roll across miles and miles of white sheet to get there. Her mouth felt dry, which woke her up a little. She was in her room, now. There was another bed in here, but it was empty. Brady had ice chips, all ready to hold out to her in a little paper cup.

"Mm," she said, as she took them.

"I'd better pick up the girls."

"Kiss them."

"I will. Can I kiss you?"

"If you like kissing sandpaper."

"I love it." He touched his mouth to hers, quick and soft. "I keep a piece in my wallet just to remind me of you."

Her laugh woke up, and she dragged her eyes open again so she could get a fresh image of him to hold in her mind.

"I want to talk later, Brady," she said.

"So do I."

By three o'clock, when the girls came, she felt much better. Still sleepy and dry-mouthed, but strong enough to fight it, with limbs light enough that she could keep bringing the melting ice chips to her lips.

Scarlett and Colleen didn't understand why Mommy was in bed, why she looked sleepy like it was night-time, and why they mustn't jump on her stomach. But they were good. So cute. Hugged her and kissed her a lot, especially Colleen. Scarlett was much more shy about it.

Because I've held back just that little bit, Libby knew. This time, I'm the one who's set the bad pattern. I have to change that. She can't call me Mommy and still feel she doesn't belong in my arms every bit as much as Colleen does.''

''I brought a couple of stories if you wanted to read to them,'' Brady said. ''And I brought… Well, the obvious.''

Flowers. He'd put them down on her meal tray, which was pushed back against the wall, and she hadn't seen them. They were gorgeous, a huge bunch of them in all the soft, pretty colors that she loved. Pink and white and yellow and purple.

''I love the obvious,'' she said. ''And I'd love to read to the girls, as long as we can stop every page or two for ice.''

The hour passed quickly, but there was no real chance to talk. It would have to wait. They both wanted it, though. When Brady squeezed her hand and she squeezed back, and when he leaned over the bed and kissed her dry lips once more, they were both silently promising, ''Later.''

Brady took the girls back to the motel for a swim in the indoor pool. Libby missed all three of them as soon as they'd gone. She wanted to sleep away the time until Brady came for her tomorrow morning—

that would be their first real chance, wouldn't it?—
but perversely now her body wouldn't cooperate. The
dryness in her mouth wouldn't go away, her limbs
felt achy and restless, and her hurting abdomen told
her that pain medication was due.

She distracted herself with television instead, and
was allowed a little soup for her evening meal, with
Jell-O for dessert. She couldn't believe it when she
saw Brady in the doorway at a quarter of nine.

"Where are the girls? They're not with you? Did
Angie—?"

"Your mom's here now, remember?" he said.
"She rescheduled her flight for forty-eight hours
later, and got to the motel half an hour ago. The girls
are asleep, and she's sitting with them. She wanted
me to come over right away. Wouldn't take no for
an answer. Told me she'd realized that if I meant
what I said about there being the slightest chance
to—" He stopped suddenly.

"What, Brady?"

He ran his fingers across the day's growth of stubble on his jaw. "Can I sit on the bed?"

"As long as it's not on my stomach. I'll scoot
over." She eased herself across carefully and he
pulled a nearby chair closer so he could sit beside
her and still have somewhere to rest his feet. She felt
nervous for some reason.

As if this was a date.

Or a crisis meeting.

"Do you remember what you were talking about
before you went under?" he asked.

"My parents' divorce."

"And your dad. Something about Disney World,
and your dad. You said that you'd said it. 'Horseback

riding and Disney World.' And then you never saw
him again.''

"Oh, yeah, that. Oh, lord! I never told Mom. Because of the 'let's wait' thing. I knew that's what she
would have said, although I didn't understand why,
back then.''

"I'm still not quite getting this, Lib.''

"I know.'' She reached out and took his hand.
Found his eyes and smiled. She loved his eyes. "I'm
getting there, okay?''

"Okay.'' He stroked the back of her hand with the
ball of his thumb, his face watchful. She refused to
let herself be daunted by the watchfulness.

"You see, I wanted Dad and me to have something to do together, the times I went for access visits,'' she said. "I was so sure it would help, and, you
know, I was twelve, with twelve-year-old-girl ideas
about what would be fun. So I thought, we'll take
up horseback riding, and we'll go to Disney World.''

"Sounds good.''

"It was. I thought. I was so pleased with myself
for finding an answer. And I suggested it, and I
waited. 'We'll see, Lisa-Belle,' he said. And I
thought, well, grown-ups say that. They don't jump
into things. And I went home from the visit. Didn't
say anything to Mom. I thought, Dad'll argue the
case better. If it comes from Dad, she'll say yes. Next
vacation got closer. Nothing got said. Two weeks
away. Nothing. You know, I'd need clothes and stuff.
Riding helmet, maybe. A new swimsuit. I wanted to
know.''

"Sure.''

"Am I looking forward to this, horseback riding
and Disney World with my dad? Maybe two weeks

this time? Or is it going to be the same awkward week, like we've been having for four years, when Mom puts me on a plane and then he and I don't know how to relate? Finally asked Mom. What's happening with vacation? With Dad? I didn't mention the ideas I'd had. She said she'd had a call from him, like, weeks ago, two or three months.''

''That long?''

''Yes, and they'd talked, and he'd said he thought it would be best if we didn't see each other anymore. She hadn't known how to tell me. I think, as usual, she'd needed time to process it herself. I—you know, I knew she wasn't strong, emotionally. I never told her how much it, oh, *killed* me, really. Killed a part of me. He died pretty suddenly, when I was eighteen. Heart attack. You know, high-pressure alpha type, never had time to look after himself. So I never got to—never got to—never—''

''Okay. It's okay.'' He slid closer, along the edge of the bed, and held her.

''It's not. It's not okay.'' She stopped trying to push back the tears. ''It never has been. I'm so angry with him! For never understanding how much he hurt me. For not trying to keep me in his life. For making me so afraid of talking to the people I love about what I need from them. You know, I told him what I needed, and he just turned his back. Forever. And I'm so, *so* angry with him for dying so we never had a chance to get over it!''

''I know, sweetheart. I know.''

''I mean, for a long time I forgave Glenn every-thing…really, at heart, it's still forgiven…because at least he—this is crazy!—at least he was *there,* so *there,* with all that confidence about his needs and mine. And he let me be there with him while he was dying, and it meant we could get closer. And we did. It wasn't perfect, but we could finish things and say goodbye. I'll never have that with Dad. I'll never get to yell at him. I'll never get to hug him.''

"Yell at me, Lib. Please?'' His voice cracked. "Hug me. Don't— You know, that's all I want. All the times when we mess things up, I just want you to stop saying, 'I'm fine.' Stacey lied to me all the time. 'I'm fine' is a different kind of lie, but it's still a lie.''

"Like silence…''

"Yeah, like silence. Lies have a lot of power. Don't do it. I'm not going to turn my back. I thought it was all about Glenn, but I was wrong. It's about your dad. I'm not *ever* going to turn my back like he did, Libby.''

"I think I've been afraid, in my heart, to get too close to Scarlett, to let her love me the way I love her, in case our marriage broke up and I ended up doing the same to her. I kept thinking that her relationship with Colleen was the one that really counted, the one we had to work on. I love her so much, but I haven't let her be my child, the way Colleen is—you know, the outfits, you were right about that—because every little increment in how she…'' She stopped and tried again. "Like when she started calling me Mommy… Every little thing made me more scared of what might happen later on. And I've been protecting Colleen in the same way. Making sure she stayed closer to me, and not so close to you. When you challenged me about the job, I thought I was defending my independence, after what I went through with Glenn, but in my heart I wasn't.

I was trying to protect both of them from getting hurt if an adult walked out on them.''

There was a knock at the door, and Libby sat up a little in the bed to see Dr. Crichton standing there.

''Hi!'' she said. ''Just come to check you out and tell you a couple of things. See if you have any questions. Sorry I couldn't make it earlier, but everything's been happening at once around here. How are you feeling?''

''Oh, I'm fi—'' Libby stopped, and flashed a quick sideways glance at Brady. ''I'm a little sore,'' she said. ''Mouth's still dry. And I'm looking forward to tomorrow when I can eat some real food.''

''Not big on the lime Jell-O, huh?'' Anne Crichton picked up her chart out of the clear plastic rack at the foot of the bed, and studied it. ''Lookin' good,'' she said. ''I'll stop by again in the morning, and if your chart still looks like this, you can leave.''

''Will I need a prescription for some pain medication?''

''We'll give you one. A lot of women find they don't need to take all of the tablets, as the pain tapers off pretty fast. You'll get some instructions from the nurse about how to look after yourself at home, and you'll get a couple of leaflets, as well. Just rest and take things easy, okay? Get everyone else to do the work!'' She smiled at Brady, and Libby realized she hadn't made introductions.

''Yes, this is my—my husband, Brady,'' she said quickly. She heard her own stumble over the words, and realized she didn't yet know if all the things they'd talked about tonight were enough to save their marriage and set it onto a better track.

''It's nice to meet you, Brady,'' Dr. Crichton said.

"And it reminds me of something I meant to say before the surgery, Libby. You may want to review your method of contraception. I'm happy to talk about it with you. You may well achieve a pregnancy very easily, now, but you should let your body fully heal from the surgery first, so you should work out what you want to do about that."

Brady cleared his throat. "Uh, not wanting to jump the gun, or anything, but when would it be safe for us to start trying? That is, if we decided we wanted to."

He looked at Libby, and then quickly away. Her heart began to beat faster.

"I'd advise waiting around three months." The doctor smiled, stacked the chart back in its holder and said, "Hope that doesn't sound too long for you, Mr. Buchanan!"

"Not as long as we can practise our technique in the meantime."

Dr. Crichton laughed, then said, "Think about any other questions you might have, Libby, and I'll answer them in the morning, okay? I have a delivery to get to, now, and if I don't make tracks, the baby's going to get there before I do."

She left the room, a cheerful whirlwind of warm energy.

"She's nice," Brady said.

"Forget that," Libby said, feeling a little shaky. "Brady, you asked her about when it would be safe to try for a baby. You—"

"Not if you don't want," he said slowly. "Maybe I shouldn't have asked. I was getting too far ahead."

"Ahead of what? I didn't even know if you still thought we had a marriage. And as for a baby—"

"I love you, Lib," he said. "I'd love to have a baby with you. Or a few babies. I love you. That's all."

"That's *all?*" She had tears in her eyes again. "That's everything, Brady! That's everything I need and want. I love you. I never thought I'd dare to love anyone like this."

"I've felt it for so long," Brady said. "But I've been so angry, too. I couldn't admit, even to myself, that I felt this way about you."

His voice was low and fast, some of his phrases a little clumsy. Libby was used to that. Loved it not only because it was part of who he was, but because it said so much about his honor and his honesty. He didn't like putting his feelings into words, but he had learned to do it when it was important.

"I couldn't accept it," he went on.

She couldn't see his face properly, because he was looking down to where their fingers tangled together. She leaned forward, hurting her stomach, and kissed him wherever her lips could reach—kisses that said, "Keep talking. I want to hear every word of this."

"There was so much in the way. Kept thinking it was going to be a saga of dishonesty and miscommunication like it was with Stacey. I didn't want to go through that again. I told myself I'd cut my losses if things didn't improve. I knew it would hurt, but I didn't realize how much until I found out about the surgery, and that you hadn't even told me. I knew right away that I had to come up here. And that I loved you with everything in me. I knew this was our last chance, and there were times when I thought it was a pretty slender one."

"Oh, Brady," she whispered, and kissed him some more. He kissed her back, hot and hard.

"But we can do this, now," he said, holding her. "We can love each other, stay together, be together."

"Tell me again. Could you? Tell me. And kiss me..."

"I love you, Lib. Give me forever."

"I'll give you forever," she answered. "The two of us. The four of us. The five or six of us, maybe someday. You and our children. Forever in my heart."

* * * * *

*We hope you love
BALANCING ACT
so much that you share it with friends
and family. If you do—or if you belong
to a book club—there are questions on
the next pages that are intended to help
you start a book group discussion. We
hope these questions inspire you and
help you get even more out of the book.*

READERS' RING DISCUSSION GROUP QUESTIONS:

1. Libby and Brady are brought together by what seems like an amazing stroke of fate. Now that adoption records are opening up, there have been lots of similar stories of miraculous coincidences in the lives of adopted children and their birth parents, or siblings and half siblings separated by adoption—a brother and sister living two blocks from each other for years without knowing of their relationship, or a birth mother admiring the achievements of a local celebrity and then discovering that he was her grown-up son.

Do you know of any inspiring stories like these?

And what would you do if you were Brady and Libby?

2. Brady and Libby attempt to create a blended family—a task that a lot of couples face today. For a long time, it doesn't quite work but they resolve their problems in the end.

Have you had any experience of blended families? Do you have any insights into how to make them work?

3. What's going on with Libby and the housework? In much of the book, she's using it at least in part as a way to hide from some deeper issues and avoid a confrontation with Brady. She feels that if she does her part in that area, she'll deflect a challenge from him over the things that aren't working.

Once their problems are resolved, do you think Libby's going to relax a little? Or is her energy around the house a positive and ingrained part of her nature? Is Brady flexible on the issue?

True confession time now, ladies. Is your house
a) immaculate and sparkling? You're a total clean freak and proud of it.
b) semi-immaculate and semi-sparkling? You kind of wish you were an (a) but just can't quite get there because of the kids/the dog/your job.
c) clean enough to be healthy? In the bits that show, anyhow.
d) Um, lets just say you have other priorities. Your mantra is "Dull women have immaculate houses," and people had better get in the habit of chanting it when they come to your place.

4. Brady and Libby are poles apart in some areas, and this is shown very early on in the scene where

he's clumsy with her little soap arrangement. Is it a case of "opposites attract" or are Libby and Brady drawn together through similarities and differences that make for the most lasting happiness in a marriage? Is it different for every couple, or are there some universal rules?

In a good romance novel, we get a unique insight into what attracts two people to each other, both physically and emotionally. That's one of the reasons that romance is so rewarding to read. In life, sometimes it's harder to understand what two people see in each other. Do you know any couples like that? "I mean, him? With her? Who'd have thought of that, in a million years!" In answering this question, names can be changed to protect true identities.

And which celebrity couple do you think is
a)   most likely to split up in the next six months?
b)   most likely to stay the full distance?
c)   most jaw-droppingly unsuited to each other?
d)   next on the list to announce that she's pregnant?
e)   only faking an involvement to publicize their latest movie?

5.   From the first moment of their physical connection to each other, Libby and Brady's relationship is a success in bed, offering both them and the reader a powerful hope that they'll be able to solve the problems that drive them apart in other areas.

Do you think good sex is always a positive element in a relationship? A place where honesty always comes through? Or can it, as Brady sometimes fears, be used as "wallpapering"—a way to cover up or hide from underlying problems? What has been your experience?

6. *Balancing Act* is a very emotional book, yet there are moments of humor and lightness that come through. Did these moments strengthen the book? Or did they distract from the serious issues that Brady and Libby were facing?

What is your own attitude toward humor at dark times in your life? Are you always able to find something to laugh about? Or is it sometimes just too hard? Is it true that laughter can heal?

7. *Balancing Act* contains several complex emotional threads. Other subjects for discussion:
a) The issue of Vietnam. How important do you think it is for Libby and Brady to keep the Vietnamese connection in their daughters' lives?
b) The question of past relationships. Libby has been more deeply scarred than Brady by her past relationships, both with her father and with her first husband, Glenn. Why do you think this is so?
c) Libby's need for secrecy. She's aware that it's potentially destructive and struggles to overcome her blocks, but takes a long time to succeed. What's your attitude to honesty in a relationship? Does everything need to be laid out on the table? Or can silence sometimes work better?
d) The settings and seasons used in the story. How are these used to reflect the emotions Libby and Brady are feeling?

e)   The writing style. How would you describe this author's work to someone who hadn't read her before? Where are her greatest strengths? What didn't work for you?

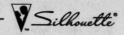

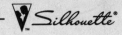

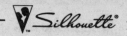

If you enjoyed what you just read,
then we've got an offer you can't resist!

Take 2 bestselling love stories FREE!

Plus get a FREE surprise gift!

Clip this page and mail it to Silhouette Reader Service™

IN U.S.A.	IN CANADA
3010 Walden Ave.	P.O. Box 609
P.O. Box 1867	Fort Erie, Ontario
Buffalo, N.Y. 14240-1867	L2A 5X3

YES! Please send me 2 free Silhouette Special Edition® novels and my free surprise gift. After receiving them, if I don't wish to receive anymore, I can return the shipping statement marked cancel. If I don't cancel, I will receive 6 brand-new novels every month, before they're available in stores! In the U.S.A., bill me at the bargain price of $3.99 plus 25¢ shipping and handling per book and applicable sales tax, if any*. In Canada, bill me at the bargain price of $4.74 plus 25¢ shipping and handling per book and applicable taxes**. That's the complete price and a savings of at least 10% off the cover prices—what a great deal! I understand that accepting the 2 free books and gift places me under no obligation ever to buy any books. I can always return a shipment and cancel at any time. Even if I never buy another book from Silhouette, the 2 free books and gift are mine to keep forever.

235 SDN DNUR
335 SDN DNUS

Name	(PLEASE PRINT)	
Address	Apt.#	
City	State/Prov.	Zip/Postal Code

* Terms and prices subject to change without notice. Sales tax applicable in N.Y.
** Canadian residents will be charged applicable provincial taxes and GST.
All orders subject to approval. Offer limited to one per household and not valid to current Silhouette Special Edition® subscribers.
® are registered trademarks of Harlequin Books S.A., used under license.

SPED02   ©1998 Harlequin Enterprises Limited

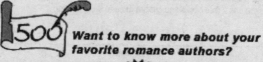

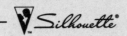

COMING NEXT MONTH

#1555 DANIEL'S DESIRE—Sherryl Woods
The Devaneys
Though he hadn't expected a second chance at happiness, that's
exactly what Daniel Devaney got when he came face-to-face
with his ex, Molly Creighton. Though a tragic loss had torn
them asunder, *this* time Daniel was determined to fight for the
love that burned stronger than ever.

#1556 PRINCE AND FUTURE...DAD?—Christine Rimmer
Viking Brides
The princess was pregnant! And the king had every intention
of making sure his daughter married the father of her unborn
child. But Princess Liv Thorson had other plans, and they didn't
include marrying the notorious playboy Prince Finn. Or so she
told herself....

#1557 QUINN'S WOMAN—Susan Mallery
Hometown Heartbreakers
Ex-Special Forces agent Quinn Reynolds agreed to share his
skills with self-defense instructor D. J. Monroe. But their sessions
triggered as many sparks as punches. Fighting the
love growing between them might only be a losing battle!

#1558 MARRY ME...AGAIN—Cheryl St.John
Montana Mavericks: The Kingsleys
Ranch foreman Devlin "Devil" Holmes had wild ways not even
getting married could tame...until Brynna decided to leave him.
Being without her was torture. Could he convince Brynna their
marriage deserved a second chance?

#1559 THE FERTILITY FACTOR—Jennifer Mikels
Manhattan Multiples
Nurse Lara Mancini struggled with the possibility that she
might be infertile. But her feelings for handsome Dr. Derek Cross
were quickly escalating. Would he want to pursue a relationship
knowing she might be unable to conceive?

#1560 FOUND IN LOST VALLEY—Laurie Paige
Seven Devils
He wasn't who she thought he was. Seth Dalton, successful
attorney, wasn't *really* a Dalton. Amelia Miller was a good
woman who deserved a good man, not a fraud. The fact that he
was falling for her didn't change a thing...but her love for him—
that could be enough to change *everything*.

SSECNM0703